Burke and the Pimpernel Affair

Tom Williams

ISBN: 978-1-8383975-5-5
First published by Big Red 2022

Contents

JAMES FLORENCE BURKE

Born Ireland 1771
Enlisted Regiment of Dillon (France). Saw active service in Sainte Domingue. Surrendered to British in 1793
Detached for special duties at the War Office
1793/4: confidential duties in Ireland
1798: confidential duties in Egypt
1805: confidential duties in Argentina
1806: attached to British forces in Buenos Aires
1806: promoted to Captain
1807: confidential mission to the Spanish court
1808: promoted to Major
1808: diplomatic posting to Brazil
1809: diplomatic posting to Argentina
1809: attached to General Hill in Spain
1809: confidential work in France
1815: confidential work with Allied occupation forces in Paris
1815: attached to the Hussars of Croy. Saw action at Waterloo

For those who like to keep track of these things, the action in this book takes place in 1809 and follows directly on from the end of *Burke in the Peninsula*. Like all the Burke stories, the book is a stand-alone novel and you can enjoy it even if you haven't read any of the others.

CHAPTER 1: Office of the Minister of Police, Paris

It was a necklace, bought in a vain attempt to impress a woman, that sealed the innkeeper's fate. Fouché held it now, sliding it through his fingers like a rosary. It glittered in the afternoon light that came in through the narrow window. It was glass, of course, and even the most ignorant Paris guttersnipe could hardly be expected to believe it was diamonds. Such a tawdry thing to put yourself in peril for.

Of course, the landlord of 'The Sign of the Doves' had no reason to think that anybody would notice something as insignificant as his purchase of a necklace. Fouché allowed himself a small smile. Foolish man! Women would threaten their children that if they misbehaved Fouché would hear of it. His network of spies extended across the whole of France. How could this Jean-Luc not realise that the most trivial things done in Paris would be brought to his attention?

Not everything, of course. There were over half a million people living in Paris. Even the Minister of Police could not be expected to watch all of them. But the landlord of an inn with a name like 'The Sign of the Doves' – that was different. The name alone condemned it. It was an old name: a name from before the revolution. Naturally this made it a hotbed of Royalists and therefore a place to be watched. And when the landlord was suddenly out buying jewellery – even cheap trash like this – one had to ask the question: where did the money come from? Not from honest profits from the inn. Most people knew better than to associate with Royalists and every year the place had fewer customers. By now the landlord should be struggling to survive, saving every centime, not out buying jewellery, presumably in the hope of enticing some woman to be his mistress. And how could he afford a mistress? By taking money from the Royalists. How else?

Fouché had had one of his men keep the place under surveillance until there was a visitor from out of town. He was from the Vendôme from his accent – that haunt of counter-revolutionaries. A routine check showed him to be travelling as Phillipe Bruit. Fouché's agent reported that the fellow lay low, not ever leaving the inn. He seemed to be waiting for someone, so Fouché waited too. And then, after a week, the second man arrived.

Fouché glanced at his agent's report. Not that he needed to look at it again: he had the details clear in his mind.

Bruit rushes out, greets second subject like a brother then looks suspiciously around before he leads him into the inn. I wait half an hour before entering and demanding his papers. They say he's Marc Duran, a wine merchant travelling up from Bordeaux. I ask if there's any chance of buying a cask for some good citizens. We were planning a party, I said. 'All gone,' he says. 'What about your mate?' I say. 'Who?' he says. 'This Phillipe. Staying here. Aren't you together?' 'No,' he says. 'Never seen him before in my life.'

It was enough. They had arrested both the men and the innkeeper for good measure. They brought in the serving girl too. She might well be innocent, but it did no harm to question her.

He would question them that night. He had much to do – France did not run itself. There were those who thought Napoleon ran it. Fouché would always agree with them but he never really believed it. The Corsican was a brilliant general, certainly, and had some wonderful ideas, but he bored easily. Somebody had to keep on top of the detail once the Emperor's mind had turned elsewhere. And Fouché considered that he was the man to do that.

He reached for another of the reports on his desk. So many reports! But it was his mastery of so much detail that had made him the power he was. He read all the reports from the regional *prefects* and produced a digest of the juiciest bits that went to Napoleon every morning. The Emperor read it religiously. He liked to be kept informed – and it was Fouché who decided exactly what he would be informed of.

It was after midnight when he finished writing his summary for Bonaparte. His pen was getting scratchy. The quill needed sharpening. No matter: once he had left his bureau someone would come in and refill the ink wells and sharpen the quills. He liked a neat office.

The prisoners would be tired by now. Tired and frightened. It was a good time to start the questioning.

Fouché decided to begin with the girl.

* * *

Sofie was, as far as she knew, just nineteen. Her parents had introduced her to the inn-keeper when times were hard five or six years ago. His wife had died and he needed somebody to fetch and carry and keep the place clean, he said. And provide entertainment for his customers, Fouché suspected, but that was neither here nor there. The gendarmes weren't sure what to make of her, but they expressed the view that there was a real chance that she was innocent.

She was sitting at a table. This was to be a civilised discussion, after all. Fouché had a sentimental reluctance to use violence on women if it could possibly be avoided. The clubs and the knives and the hot pokers, if they were to be used at all, would come later.

She looked up as he entered the room.

"Why do you walk funny?"

Fouché had a club foot. It made him walk with a peculiar swaying gait and the clump, clump of the deformed foot on floorboards usually gave notice of his arrival. It generally scared people, which Fouché considered useful. He pretended not to care about that foot, but he did. People around him knew not to mention it. But this girl did not know him and, perhaps because she didn't recognise his reputation, she was not afraid. So instead of asking his first question, here he was answering it.

"I was born with a defect of my foot."

"I'm sorry."

"It is nothing." He sat down himself and made an effort to clear his mind: to concentrate on the business at hand. But it was no use. The interview had got away from him before it had even begun. He asked a few formal questions and had her sent back to her cell. His gut told him that she was innocent, but he would question her again tomorrow, just to be sure. There was no hurry. She wasn't going anywhere.

Next came Marc Duran. Fouché remained in his seat while Duran was escorted in.

Fouché's men had found a vintner somewhere in the warren of government offices where the Minister of Police squatted like a club-footed spider, spinning his web to catch spies and counter-revolutionaries and possible enemies of the Emperor Napoleon. The Emperor liked to keep a good cellar and the vintner knew his trade. It took him less than ten minutes with the man calling himself Duran before he had been able to confirm that the prisoner was almost entirely ignorant of the wine trade.

"We know you are not a wine merchant."

Duran stuck to his story.

"I am. The old man tricked me with his stupid questions."

Fouché sat quietly while the prisoner carried on with his rubbish about being a wine merchant. He wasn't really even listening. It helped, sometimes, to let prisoners talk themselves out.

Once the man had stopped gabbling his nonsense, Fouché tried again. "I am not going to believe your story. Even if it were true, I would not believe it. So tell me something else. Make something up. Lie to me. You have nothing to lose."

He watched Duran trying to think through what Fouché had said. He was offering him a way out. He just wanted him to start talking about anything other than his ridiculous lies about being a merchant. But Duran, it seemed, was too stupid to take the opportunity. He was, he insisted once more, a vintner.

Fouché sent him back to his cell. He would talk to him again tomorrow, and the day after if need be. Most people responded eventually. Only the very stupid or the very brave had to be tortured into confessions. With this Marc Duran, Fouché suspected he might end up resorting to violence but he would try a more cerebral approach first.

The innkeeper came next.

This Fouché considered, was a more productive interview. The innkeeper was no fool and he knew his best hope was to tell his interrogator all he knew. Unfortunately, he knew very little. It was as Fouché had suspected. 'The Sign of

3

the Doves' had been struggling. Every year he had fewer customers. When he had been offered a handsome payment to shelter people in his inn – people whose papers might not be entirely in order, people who shouldn't appear on any records he handed over to the gendarmerie – he had accepted.

"Who made you the offer?"

Nobody he knew: someone who had heard of the inn and the sort of people who drank there.

He gave a description willingly enough. Unlike Duran, he recognised that the best way of coming out of this alive was to be as helpful as he could be. He told Fouché of everybody who had passed through the inn. He gave names; he gave descriptions. The trouble was that the names were all undoubtedly aliases and the descriptions were generally along the lines of: "Tall fellow, brown hair; bit skinny." Still, it was better than nothing. Fouché's skill lay in putting scraps of information together until he had something useful.

"Where did they come from?"

"They never said. Their accents were from all over the place."

"But how did they get to you? Did they travel alone or in groups? Did they ride? Did they have baggage?"

Usually two or three at a time, he said. Always on foot. Sometimes they carried baggage, other times packages were delivered to them by a carrier.

"Tell me about the carrier."

"I never saw him. They'd tell me to take a walk. I'd close the place – they paid me well enough – and he'd come while I was out."

"And you never tried to sneak a look?"

The man looked shifty: embarrassed even. Fouché never ceased to marvel at the way that people would happily admit to treason or sometimes even murder and then be ashamed to admit they had told a petty lie to a friend.

He had sneaked a look, of course, but his description of man (middle height, brown hair) and cart ("just a regular cart") didn't really help.

In the end the simplest thing to do with the innkeeper seemed to be to send him back to his inn with a clear indication of what would happen to him if he had any new visitors who weren't reported direct to Fouché's office. A baited trap, he always thought, was more useful than stopping up the holes where the counter-revolutionaries hid out.

* * *

Fouché had left Phillipe Bruit until last. The man had claimed to be a painter and, left alone with some water colours, he had produced some nice little pictures. Fouché looked forward to the interview. Spies were often painters: the ability to produce accurate pictures of fortifications and gun emplacements – or even just terrain and roads – was useful in intelligence work. The interview should be a challenge.

After half an hour Fouché had confirmed to his own satisfaction that the man was a trained agent. There were tiny traces of an English accent when he got excited and a little less careful in his speech. He could even have been English, though he must have lived some time in France. More likely, Fouché thought, that he was one of Wyndham's agents: a Royalist who had fled to London and been recruited through the infernal Alien Office to be trained by the English until he could be used to attack his own country. The English were pigs to behave like that: worse than the traitors they nourished. Taking people and turning them against the land that had given them birth. It was contemptible.

For Fouché the interrogation was a game. He felt, too that it was a game for the agent. He played along, answering all the questions he was asked with an apparently sincere desire to help. Where had he come from? From Saint-Brice-sous-Ranes. No, he knew nobody in Paris who could vouch for that. Perhaps Citizen Fouché would care to send a message to the mayor there, who would be happy to confirm his identity?

Fouché smiled at that. Days for a messenger to get there, days for him to get back, and then quite possibly questions about the man's description or details of who his parents were supposed to be. It was all about slowing down his investigation, buying time for the English to warn their other agents, allowing them to hide or flee.

The man was good. The interview was proving as amusing as Fouché had hoped, but definitely less informative.

It was almost three in the morning. He would achieve nothing more tonight.

"Take him away," he ordered. "Stick him in a cell with the other one. Let us see if fear is contagious."

Later, he realised he should have stopped earlier. He had been too tired. He had made a stupid error.

* * *

That night the painter – Fouché was sure the name he had given was false and he never discovered his real one – strangled his companion. He had then cut his own throat with a small blade he had concealed in the heel of his shoe.

Fouché did not lose his temper on hearing the news. Losing one's temper was a sign of weakness. But the jailer was transferred to be the turnkey in Iles des Saintes where his chances of dying of one tropical fever or another should relieve the State of the cost of his pension.

The deaths were a setback. But 'The Sign of the Doves' was now watched. The carter could be intercepted if he called again. It would all take time, but Fouché considered there was no hurry. He would bide his time. He would track the paths of these traitors back to their lair and then he would have the whole pack of them.

5

CHAPTER 2: Merida, Spain

James Burke yawned, stretched and rolled out of bed. The sun was already ridiculously bright. It looked set to be another lovely day in Merida.

He pulled on his red coat. This, he told himself, was what he had always wanted: to be an officer in His Majesty's Army. No more skulking around spying for Colonel Gordon. No more sneaking up on the enemy in the dark, cutting throats and disappearing into the night. He wore the King's uniform again, ready to face the French on the field of battle.

Why, then, did he feel so dissatisfied with life?

The truth was, he was bored. He wasn't facing the enemy on the field of battle. He'd missed the fighting at Talavera and the retreat back towards Portugal had not been glorious at all. Every day they buried more men dead of their wounds; every day men collapsed from hunger, unable to march any further.

At least there was food now that they had regrouped just short of the Portuguese border. The French seemed to be in no hurry to attack, so the troops had had a chance to rest and recover from their march westward. Rations were still barely adequate, but food arrived more often than not and days would pass when nobody died at all.

There was nothing glorious about life in Merida though. He had been attached to General Hill's staff, but the general did not really have anything for him to do. Nobody really had anything to do. There were requisitions to be written out, of course, and various returns on the numbers of troops. Someone in the Army or, more likely, safe back in London was desperately concerned about numbers. The trouble was that numbers were constantly changing as men fell sick or died and others recovered and were returned to their units from being nursed in the villages around or even, for some of the most severely injured, from hospital in Badajoz.

His fellow officers were polite, but often distant. All recognised that he was on attachment, his own regiment fighting in the Netherlands, so the comradeship engendered by the British regimental system was not there for him. Worse, rather too many realised that he was not a regular soldier. He was not even one of Wellington's scouts. (He still thought of the newly elevated Viscount as Wellesley, but he was training himself out of the habit.) The scouts might adventure into enemy territory but they at least did it in uniform. No, rumour had it that he was one of the government's confidential agents, little better than a damn spy. It made people nervous. Burke wondered how much more nervous they would be if they knew how much dirty work he had done for the government since the Wars with France had started.

At least people appreciated his fluency in Spanish and recognised that he could be charming when required. That meant he spent much of his time dealing with the locals who had had officers billeted on them. Most of the Spaniards had been happy enough with the payments that they were promised for looking after their uninvited guests, but the government back in England was slow to send the gold General Wellington had been told was on its way. With no money in the Army's war chests, all that could be offered to their landlords was assurances that cash would be arriving soon. The goodwill of the natives was, unsurprisingly, wearing thin.

Burke made his way downstairs where his own landlady, Senora Cubero, had set out some bread and salami for his breakfast. There were no problems with his rent. Bored officers gamble and James Burke was an accomplished card player. His winnings were more than enough to satisfy Sra Cubero.

As he ate, he wondered how he would fill his day. It was understood that nobody turned up at regimental headquarters before noon. His fellow officers would not appreciate any undue diligence from him.

A few hundred gold sovereigns had arrived at Merida a few days earlier. There was little left after some attempt had been made to pay off the regiment's debts to local tradesmen, but there had been enough for Burke to spread some gold around the billets, so he did not anticipate the need to placate landlords today.

He wondered about visiting William Brown. His sergeant had been an invaluable companion through his adventures in espionage but, now they were both attached to Hill's forces, Brown had been assigned duties as a regular NCO. Unlike Burke, he had fought at Talavera and since then his men would follow him anywhere. Burke knew he would be fully occupied chasing down any extra rations he could find so his platoon was always fed well, ensuring that the wooden cabins they had built for shelter were kept clean and sound, and finding occupation to keep them out of trouble. While the men of other platoons still sulked around their camp, clearly bitter with the remembrance of the march back from Talavera, Brown's boys (as several of the officers had taken to calling them) stood out as amongst the most battle-ready of Hill's force.

No, Brown was busy in his own place in the Army and would not appreciate Major Burke trespassing in his domain.

Sra Cubero bustled in with a second cup of coffee. It was good coffee but the unmistakeable message of all that bustling was that Major Burke should be out of the house and let her be about her business. Burke sighed and raised the coffee to his lips.

* * *

He dawdled as much as he could. He took a turn around the town, but a circuit of the whole place – little more than an overgrown village – took him scarcely half an hour. None of his fellow officers were up and about, so he could not even turn the morning to advantage by taking a few guineas off them at cards.

He found himself drifting towards the little settlement of wooden huts that the troops had thrown up to shelter from the sun. There had been scarcely any rain in the month since they arrived, but Burke doubted that the shacks would provide much protection once December came. Still, with any luck they would have moved on by then. Surely they could not be planning to over-winter here?

Truth to tell, the war seemed to have ground to a halt, at least as far as Wellington's army was concerned. Burke realised that his steps were taking him towards the huts where Sgt Brown's platoon was quartered. He pulled himself up sharply. This would not do! He turned and headed towards General Hill's office. It must be almost noon by now. He might as well show his face there.

He was, as he had feared, the first officer to arrive at the old farmhouse Hill had adopted as his headquarters. To his surprise, the sergeant who, despite Hill's array of *aides de camp*, actually ran the general's office, told him that Hill had already been asking for him.

His first thought was that he must be in some sort of trouble, but he could not imagine how. Since arriving in the peninsula he had seduced no wives, insulted no husbands and engaged in no dubious trading in valuables of uncertain provenance. He had, indeed, been a model of probity. Perhaps one of his fellow officers had complained about how much he had lost at cards, but that seemed unlikely. Aside from Burke himself, there was scarcely a soul who had not had weeks when he had near bankrupted himself at the card table, but that was generally regarded as an inevitable part of Army life.

So it was with a clear conscience, but an uneasy feeling that he might have forgotten something, that Burke knocked on Hill's door.

'Daddy' Hill waved him to a seat. "Ah, Burke." He searched among the papers on his desk and lifted one triumphantly. "Here it is." He read it through quickly, as if checking he'd got the right one and pushed it across to Burke.

"It looks as if you are leaving us, Burke. Not enough here to keep you if, as seems likely, we're staying where we are for a while. Colonel Gordon appears quite anxious to have you back. Dark doings beside the Thames perhaps." He chuckled. "Probably should have sent a runner over with the message but as I knew you'd be here I thought I'd give you the news myself."

He stood and leaned across the desk, extending a hand to Burke. "You've done a good job, Burke. I'm sorry to see you go." Then he sat down and was once more busy with his papers. Burke, who was used by now to his abrupt ways, recognised that he had been dismissed. As he was about to leave the room, though, Hill looked up and added, "You'll need to take your man Brown with you. Get my sergeant to organise your transport. He's good at things like that."

And that, Burke thought, was that. So much for fighting in Spain; so much for wearing the uniform of the King. If Gordon was recalling him to London, he was sure that the man had some nefarious plan he wanted Burke engaged in. It would mean more dirty work, more skulduggery, more devious plots. Still, Burke thought, remembering how he had felt that morning, at least he wouldn't be bored.

He wondered what the scheming old devil had in store.

CHAPTER 3: Horse Guards, London

"Sit down, Burke. Have a brandy."

Burke sat. He would have been happier if Colonel Gordon had barked his orders in his usual abrupt way. If Gordon was drinking brandy in his office with his juniors, then something must be worrying him a lot.

"I believe that the last time you left Spain you travelled via France and crossed the Channel in the company of several barrels of brandy." Gordon swirled his glass. "Not dissimilar to this, in fact."

Burke smiled. The Army had run agents in and out of France courtesy of the 'gentlemen' who smuggled liquor into England to the despair of the Excise Officers. Some of the brandy had, unofficially but inevitably, ended up in the War Office cellars – and, Burke suspected, more than a few officers' messes.

Gordon sniffed at his brandy appreciatively. "Sadly, such days are over. The French have clamped down on smugglers and the Excise have complained that the Army is in league with them, so our happy days of freelancing across the Channel are over." He took another swallow. "I'll miss the brandy."

Burke sipped, wondering where this was going.

"You dealt with Wickham, years ago, didn't you?"

"I never met him, sir. I dealt with one of his functionaries. A Mr Smith." Burke's tone was heavily ironic. He had not liked 'Mr Smith' and he had not liked the Alien Office that employed him.

"Well, the Alien Office has gone from strength to strength. Wickham's not there anymore, of course, but Sidney Smith has got his oar in somehow."

Gordon, Burke thought, must be seriously annoyed to have neglected Sir Sidney Smith's honorific.

"The place considers itself the centre for our country's intelligence effort. Which is all well and good when they mean smuggling political leaflets into France and encouraging men to plant infernal machines in the capital, but when it comes to anything useful, they are rank amateurs. They wouldn't know an order of battle if it bit them in the arse. And when you ask for estimates of regimental strength, they just make up some number based on what they think politically expedient. Bloody aristocratic dandies, plotting and bitching and drawing up their damn pamphlets. Sometimes I think the French had the right idea getting rid of them."

Gordon paused to take another generous swig of brandy. The pause extended to the point where Burke realised that he was supposed to make some contribution of his own. He opened his mouth hesitantly. He was clearly being lured into political territory and he was anxious to stay on the right side of his chief.

"I suppose we should keep some of our own agents in play."

Gordon's smile showed that he had said the right thing.

"We should and we do. The trouble is getting them into France. The Alien Office has some chap called Wright, who has been allocated his own small fleets of cutters and luggers and – well, assorted things with sails." Gordon, it was clear, was not a naval man. In fact, like many Army officers, he harboured deep suspicions about the Navy, especially now when both services were busy blaming each other for the setbacks at Walcheren.

"Anyway, on the basis that ships are involved, the Admiralty has been put in charge, which has allowed Sir Sidney his opportunity to be the man of the hour. Hero of Acre and all that." Sidney Smith's ability to pop up in convenient places and bathe in the subsequent glory of his actions obviously rankled.

The colonel's brandy glass was empty. He refilled it.

"The Navy having the responsibility for getting men and materiel across the water wouldn't be a problem except that, because the bloody man is in with the Alien Office, the estimable Sir Sidney insists that the amateurs Wickham brought into the game should now be responsible for the movement of agents onward into France. So when I want somebody quietly inserted into a garrison town on the French border, I have to accept that he will be shuttled along some elaborate chain of safe houses. Good god! The man has even had builders in to make secret rooms in some of them."

Gordon paused again, as if contemplating the enormity of the Alien Office's folly.

"I can see it's annoying, sir, but does it do any actual harm to our activities?"

"Ah, Burke! There you hit the nail on the head." The brandy was put to one side and Gordon was all business again. "Bonaparte is regrouping after his success against Austria. Is there any danger of a push in Spain, or is everyone settling down into winter quarters? Simple question. Obvious answer: send a couple of chaps over. Hang around garrisons, buy people a few drinks, get the lie of the land. Straightforward sort of thing – you've done it often enough yourself." Burke nodded. Travelling through France, claiming to be a merchant or a land agent posed no great difficulties, provided you carried forged papers and spoke the language well enough. Hiding in plain sight was often easier than skulking from safe house to safe house, although both approaches had advantages and disadvantages. He knew that many of the agents employed by the Alien Office were amateurs – refugees who just wanted to save their country for the Bourbons. For them, the support of a network of agents across France was a vital prop. For a trained and experienced professional spy, the advantages were less obvious.

"Problem is: a few of our agents seem to have gone missing. Carried across the Channel, put safely ashore, messages saying they have passed safely along the chain as far as Paris and then nothing. We ask the Alien Office what's happened and they say they've done their bit and the fault must be our chaps being caught after Paris."

Burke allowed himself a sceptical raise of his eyebrows.

Gordon nodded. "Just so. Fact is, I'm pretty sure the Alien Office operation has been compromised. That fellow who runs their secret police ..."

"Fouché."

"Yes, that's the man. No fool. I think he's penetrated the chain of safe houses and somewhere between the coast and Paris our agents are being quietly rounded up."

"What does the Alien Office say?"

"Can't be happening. They'd know. Everything is working smoothly and if we're losing people it's our own carelessness."

There was a long silence. Gordon watched Burke, who was beginning to think he knew where this was going and wasn't happy with what he was imagining.

Gordon broke the silence. "I want you to go over and take a look."

"You want me to take the same trip that's lost us – how many men exactly?"

"Three."

"Good men?"

"Not as good as you."

That was high praise from Gordon and Burke would have been delighted in other circumstances. Now, though, he would rather Gordon had picked out some other man as the best for the job.

"I'm not sure why you think I'll get through where three others haven't."

"Because you will have the estimable Sgt Brown with you."

Gordon explained his idea. Burke thought it hardly qualified as a plan, but there were, perhaps, the faint outlines of a plan that might just work.

Brown was to be landed using the Navy's ships and passed up the line of safe houses. Burke, meanwhile, was to be put ashore by a smuggling crew that Gordon had been holding back for such an eventuality. "You didn't think I'd leave us completely at the mercy of the Navy, did you? But this is entirely *sub rosa*. As far as the Alien Office is concerned, you don't exist. So once you are ashore it is almost as important for you to keep hidden from our own side as it is from the French. That is, if they are our own side. We have no idea how far the French have penetrated our network. That's the main thing we want you to find out. Find out how far the rot goes and then cut it out."

"At my discretion."

"Absolutely at your discretion, Major. After all, as far as the War Office is concerned, you were never there. In fact –" Gordon looked thoughtful – "it's probably best if you have some sort of *nom de guerre* for this exercise. Something that won't tie you to the Army."

There was a silence while both men tried to think of something appropriate. Then Gordon spoke again. "You'll be hiding away like some sort of shrinking violet. So 'Violet' maybe."

"Perhaps something less associated with the fairer sex, sir."

"Indeed, yes. Well, if not 'Violet', how about 'Pimpernel'."

Burke had little patience with code names, but this, he thought, would do. "Very good, sir. 'Pimpernel' it is."

CHAPTER 4: On board the *Mary Jane* off the French coast

James Burke had never considered a naval career. The Army, carrying out its business on solid ground, had always seemed a much more reliable option than the Navy, at the mercy of the vagaries of wind and wave. Like most soldiers, he tended to forget that fighting the enemies of the king meant spending a surprising amount of time on ships travelling to wherever those enemies might be. He had crossed the Atlantic back and forth three times, from north to south as well as east to west. He had sailed the length of the Mediterranean and travelled from London to Lisbon and back again. He had made innumerable trips across the Channel in all sorts of vessels. Yet, despite all this maritime experience, he was still deeply suspicious of ships – and the smaller the ship, the more uncomfortable it made him.

The lugger *Mary Jane* (Burke found himself vaguely wondering who Mary Jane had been) was, he judged, less than 40 feet long. Tied up on the Cuckmere River this had seemed a reasonable size. Now, tossing in the Channel swell, it seemed ridiculously small.

The crew had nets over the side and were making a half-hearted pretence of fishing. It was, Burke thought, unlikely to convince any French patrols that came by, but it was marginally better than sitting there with no excuse at all. And there was always the possibility that they might really catch something.

Although the crew were experienced hands, Burke could feel the tension aboard. Usually ships like the *Mary Jane* would dash in and out of French waters, relying on their speed to keep them out of danger. Waiting offshore like this was not just risky but, it seemed to the crew, an unnatural risk. Yet they had little choice. Burke thought back to when this plan had been hatched. It had seemed so easy then.

* * *

The Alien Office would not share any details of how their agents, now including William Brown, were to be put ashore. "Security," one of their representatives had told Colonel Gordon. "Can't be too careful with this sort of thing." Gordon, Burke thought, must have come close to an apoplectic attack. Certainly the level of drink in his brandy bottle was noticeably lower when Burke had next called in his office to make their plans.

All Gordon knew was that Sgt Brown was to be landed near Dieppe. "And he'll be climbing cliffs. They had to tell me that because they needed to know that he would be up to it. Damn silly thing to ask about a soldier but it's a nasty climb they say."

"If they are talking about a demanding climb, then he must be going ashore north of Dieppe."

Gordon unrolled a map of the area.

"That sounds about right. He's going to be in a gun brig that the Navy uses for this sort of thing apparently. The *Basilisk*. If you hang around at sea you should be able to see where they put him ashore. It will have to be between Dieppe and Tréport. Then you can land here." Gordon peered at the map and brought his finger firmly down on the little village of Criel-sur-Mer. "Or here." He stabbed again, about five miles to the south. "Petit-Caux. Either way you shouldn't be more than four or five miles from where they land, even allowing that you won't be able to take a direct route. They'll be climbing the cliffs and not all of them will be as fit as your sergeant, so I imagine they'll take a while. By the time they're at the top you should be close enough to be able to see where they're going. There can't be many houses out there." Gordon peered again at the map which, Burke could see, suggested a great deal of empty space above the cliffs. "Should be straightforward."

Gordon had rolled up the map with the relaxed air of a man who was going to be comfortable in London while Burke was doing his dirty work. Still, Burke had thought, it wasn't a bad plan. He'd certainly known worse.

* * *

A sudden squall of wind hit the side of the *Mary Jane* and she lurched hard to the left. 'Port,' Burke corrected himself. When you were about to be tossed into the sea from an open boat, it was always good to know if you were going to drown to port or starboard.

He wondered how William Brown was faring. Crossing the Channel on the *Basilisk* he would be exposed to the worst of the elements for only the last few hundred yards to the shore.

The lugger lurched again. Burke was generally a good sailor but he was definitely getting queasy.

Squally as it was, they at least had a clear sky and just enough moonlight to have a reasonable chance of spotting the *Basilisk* when it turned up. They had positioned themselves directly between Criel-sur-Mer and Petit-Caux, so the *Basilisk* should have to pass within a couple of miles of them. In Gordon's office the idea of following Brown's trail like this had seemed so simple as to need no discussion. Now, though, Burke feared the plan could fall at this first hurdle.

Burke raised his telescope and tried to fix it on the horizon, which continued to swing up and down in a way he found more than a little disconcerting. His chances of spotting the *Basilisk* he felt were negligible: his efforts were just to show willing in front of the crew. It was the sailors he was relying on. Their ability to pick out details of the coastline in the darkness was almost preternatural and they were confident they would see William's ship in plenty of time to spot their landing point.

"Don't you worry," their captain – a ridiculously young man (at least in Burke's view) – was reassuring. "We've never had a Frenchie sneak up on us without seeing it miles off. We'll spot a gun-brig easily enough."

The ship rolled again – to starboard this time. Burke was sitting against the bulwark but his head jerked back and smacked firmly against the ship's timbers. The captain, though standing, balanced himself against the roll, his own telescope pointed unwaveringly at the horizon.

A few minutes later Burke felt him tense and then: "Haul in the nets."

Four men hauled in the nets. To Burke's surprise there was a reasonable catch, shiny silver even in the starlight. The fish were dumped unceremoniously into the boat.

"They're heading just south of us."

Burke thought of the map he had examined in Gordon's office. "Looks like we'd best head for Petit-Caux then."

"Not yet. We're going to lower sail. They're going to pass close. I want us as unnoticeable as possible. And keep quiet. Sound travels on the water."

Burke was sceptical about the chances of people hearing anything over the noise of wind and wave but then there was a sudden lull in the wind and he heard the crack of a sail clearly across the water. There was the *Basilisk*, a patch of darkness that obscured the stars, the new moon catching faintly on its sails. He watched as it passed a mile or so to the south west and then, faintly, came the sound of orders shouted, and the splash of a boat lowered to the water.

He followed the progress of the *Basilisk*'s boat as it pulled towards the shore. The cliffs, like those at Dover, were white and glowed softly in the light of the night sky. Every so often, as it crested a wave, the boat could be seen for an instant, dark against the cliff. There was a glint of light from the shore. The reception party was ready. Burke could not see the rope that ran down from the clifftop but he knew it was there. It was a dizzying climb and he did not envy William.

"Why here?" he asked the captain. "Why not at Petit-Caux?"

The man looked surprised at the question.

"You don't know?"

Burke shook his head.

"The French aren't stupid. They've got chasseurs patrolling all along this bit of coast. There'll likely be a guard at Petit-Caux."

Burke thought of Gordon's comment: "Should be straightforward." It was flattering in a way, Burke thought, that Gordon felt he would be easily able to deal with the situation. He only hoped he could justify Gordon's optimism. Otherwise it seemed likely that he was not long for this world.

The crew were already raising sail on the *Mary Jane*. "Ready about." Sails dipped and tilted, the crew moving as one to bring the *Mary Jane* onto her new course, the sails now set to catch every scrap of wind. The ship surged forward.

16

"We'll have you at Petit-Caux in no time."

Their wake phosphoresced in the water behind them and the shore grew steadily nearer. The cliffs were less steep here and ahead there was a break where they dipped down almost to the water before rising again beyond it.

"There's Petit-Caux. There's an easy track where the cliffs are low, but that's where the Frogs have likely set a guard."

Burke nodded. He was stripping his clothes off and wrapping them into a bundle that he covered with oil-cloth. There was no ship's boat on the *Mary Jane*. She would beach as close to the shore as she could and after that he was on his own.

There was a scraping sound as the lugger ran onto the sand. The sails were dropped and two of the crew were already overboard to push her clear. Burke splashed into the water alongside them and struck out for the shore. Soon he was able to feel the sand beneath his feet and half swam, half staggered through the water. Behind him he heard voices giving quiet orders, but the sound still seemed terrifyingly loud in the silence of the night. Surely any guards would be alerted by the noise. If they caught him still fighting his way ashore, his mission was over before it had begun.

He glanced over his shoulder. The lugger's sails were set again and she was already pulling away, back towards England and home. He suddenly felt very alone.

CHAPTER 5: Petit-Caux, France

He was out of the water now, with a few yards of sand between him and the cliffs. He headed toward the cliff, rather than straight into the gap, where he could see the beginning of a path upward. No point in plunging head first into trouble – especially naked as the day he was born.

Beyond the sand there was a strip of rocks and he picked his way carefully across these in his bare feet, sheltering as close to the cliff face as he could get before unwrapping his water-proofed bundle. He had put in a rough towel, with which he dried himself vigorously. The fear that he had felt crossing to shelter and the effort that he had made to get to the cliffs as fast as he could meant that he had scarcely felt the chill up to now, but once he was still he knew he was dangerously cold. He needed to be dry and the roughness of the towel brought the blood back to the surface of his skin.

He dressed quickly: breeches, shirt, a decent travelling coat and good boots. His knife was slipped into his boot. It was the only weapon he had: a sword was too unwieldly and a pistol too noisy and unreliable.

Dressed and more or less dry, he lay quiet, calming his breathing and listening for any clue as to where the guards – if there were guards – might be.

He heard boots crunching on the rocks beyond the entrance to the path. Had they left the path unguarded? Could he risk a dash to safety?

No, the boots were coming back. There was nowhere to hide. Carefully, silently, he stretched out on the ground, hoping to be lost in the darkness.

"I still think you imagined it."

My god, he thought, those voices are close. He risked lifting his head. He thought he could make out the shapes of two men walking towards him.

"There was a ship. It came right in."

"And then vanished away in the night." The voice was sceptical. "So what was it doing? There's no smugglers, no goods left on the beach for collection."

"Perhaps they put someone ashore. An English spy! You hear of such things."

The other laughed.

"You certainly hear of these things. Usually in the *Bear* after everyone has had a skin full."

"You can laugh, but we'd best keep our eyes peeled."

They were seconds away from the path. Once they had taken up position there, Burke could think of no way that he would be able to pass unseen. He had to keep them from leaving the beach.

He felt among the rocks for a stone that fit comfortably in his hand and threw it as far as he could while lying on the ground. It landed a few yards away with a satisfying clatter.

"You heard that!"

The second guard was still sceptical, but he sounded much less sure of himself.

"A fox maybe. Or just the wind."

"We should check. Over there, on the rocks."

They headed towards the spot where the stone had landed.

Now they were near enough for Burke to make them out despite the darkness. Each carried a musket. They moved cautiously forward with their weapons ready to fire.

It was a strange thing about people, Burke had noticed over years of this sort of thing. They may be hunters or hunted, but they are almost always one or the other. The two men, weapons at the ready, saw themselves as hunters. It never occurred to them that they might be prey, or that their nemesis had drawn the knife from his boot and was gliding silently across the rocks towards them.

The guards were crunching over gravel and rocks with the confidence of armed soldiers closing in on one fugitive skulking against the cliffs. One of them was probably still feeling confident when Burke's left hand reached around him, covering his mouth and pulling his head back as the right hand drew the knife sharply across his throat.

The whole thing took only seconds and happened in almost total silence, but something made the other guard turn. Foolishly, he tried to raise his musket, but Burke was already too close. The long barrel of the gun pressed uselessly against Burke's side, pointing out to sea. With both his hands holding the weapon, the guard had no way to protect himself as Burke took one step forward and drove his knife under the man's ribcage and into his gut.

He dropped the musket and looked down at the blood pouring from the wound. He seemed more surprised than anything else. Burke stepped back to avoid the blood and, with a gurgling cry that would have been unheard even a hundred yards away, the man pitched forward and died.

Burke cleaned his knife carefully before returning it to his boot and setting off up the path.

CHAPTER 6: William's journey

It felt odd to be starting a job without Major Burke.

William was used to working alone. He was proud of the fact that Major Burke trusted him to operate independently when they had to separate on a mission – but that was different from this. This time he was setting off into the unknown with only the vaguest notion of what faced him. He was to be moved like a parcel, ordered about by a bunch of civilians from the Alien Office until he reached Paris. Only, of course, if he did reach Paris, the whole thing would have been a waste of time. He was to be moved along a line of safe houses until something went wrong.

He had heard that in India they often left a goat in the forest as bait in a tiger hunt. He felt a lot like that goat.

The Alien Office had arranged for him to be collected from an inn, on the grounds that they did not want to have their operations linked to the Army, so collecting him from barracks was apparently out of the question. ("The French have spies everywhere. We can't take the risk of being seen.") He was then carried in a closed coach to Putney.

The whole cloak and dagger operation seemed to him utterly absurd but he was to realise that was the way the Alien Office went about things.

At Putney he was released from the coach and found himself in a rather elegant house on the banks of the Thames.

He wasn't supposed to know it was Putney, but he hadn't worked as an Army scout without acquiring the ability to judge distance and direction, closed coach or not. The fact that the river was visible from the house helped, as had the clattering as the carriage crossed the only bridge on that part of the Thames. It all confirmed his view that the Alien Office were amateurs when it came to this business.

He was not reassured when he was introduced to the agents who were to travel with him. There were two men, Julien and Fabrice, and one woman, Pascale. He was confident these were not their real names – but as he was travelling as Jean Baptiste he couldn't really complain about that.

Nobody talked about their business in France. William hardly expected them to. Indeed, he would have been shocked if they had. The men, though, seemed quiet by nature while Pascale was a natural chatterbox. She was in her early twenties, wearing a travelling cloak that, to William's military eye, seemed more concerned with fashion than practicality. While the men of the party wore solid woollen garments, hers was a lighter cloth lined, he thought, with silk and cut with an eye to draping elegantly over her arm as she displayed the dress below, rather than keeping out the elements.

Julien had the air of an ex-soldier and William could imagine him putting together one of the infernal machines that kept the French secret police on their toes. Ever since the attempt on Napoleon's life in 1800 had devastated a whole street in Paris, the Royalists saw bombs as their most effective weapon against Napoleon's regime. They were forever planning to lay bombs. When they were not plotting explosions there were other plots: plots to turn the Emperor's generals against each other, plots to raise revolts in the Vendôme, plots to bring remote cousins of the dead King Louis back to France to lead a counter-revolution. Not all the Royalists were directly planning acts of violence. Some were propagandists: pamphlets, written in French but printed in England, were always turning up in Paris. Gillray (who William didn't approve of because, in his opinion, Gillray's cartoons showed no respect for the monarchy) produced regular satirical prints of the French Emperor and these, too, found their way into Paris. Someone was carrying all this stuff across to France and, looking at Pascale, William thought that was probably her role.

William was conscious of appraising glances from the three of them as they, too, tried to judge what business he might have in France but nobody would admit to any unhealthy curiosity. This could have resulted in an uncomfortable silence, but Pascale filled the void with chatter about the weather and whether dresses in Paris were being worn shorter than in England and how nice it would be to see the latest fashions. The men were required only to utter occasional phrases of conventional agreement and so the social niceties were observed while they waited for the next stage of their trip.

The coach that drew up at the front door of the Putney house some twenty minutes after William's arrival was larger and more comfortable than the one that had collected him from London. The man who emerged was about forty and introduced himself as Mr Smith. William wondered how the Alien Office distinguished the various Smiths in their employ but, before he could dwell on that, Mr Smith was issuing orders in the commanding style of the military man he clearly was. In William's opinion, he had more about him of the Navy than the Army, which did nothing to improve his view of those responsible for the whole exercise.

Everybody was to be ready to leave in ten minutes. (Smith consulted a large pocket watch to emphasise the point.) They were to proceed to Portsmouth to take ship for France. Their baggage would be brought on separately. He saw Julien and Fabrice exchange a nervous look and wondered just how explosive their baggage was. Still, if there were any accidents, the gunpowder would not be sharing the coach with them.

Ten minutes later Smith was standing by the coach looking irritably at his watch while everyone waited for Pascale to do whatever it was that ladies – secret agents or not - did before they could leave the house. Julien and Fabrice fidgeted in their seats, Fabrice occasionally chewing at his knuckles. William sat back and passed the time watching Smith and wondering how angry he would be when Pascale eventually arrived.

When the woman did turn up – only five minutes late, though it must have seemed a lot longer to the others – William was impressed with Smith's restraint. He gave her a stiff half bow and remarked that punctuality was important on this journey. Pascale gave him a dazzling smile (it was the first time William had really noticed how pretty she was) and apologised. "We ladies," she said, "can't just dash out like you gentlemen," and that was that.

As soon as Pascale was settled in, Smith drew down the blinds. "It's only until we're on the road," he explained. "If things go wrong, the less you know about our operation, the better."

There was an uncomfortable silence as everybody considered the implications of that phrase "if things go wrong". Then Smith struck the coach roof in signal to the driver and they were on their way.

In keeping with the whole atmosphere of mystery that the Alien Office liked to surround itself with, they were travelling by night. This seemed madness to William. A carriage rattling down the Guildford road (Smith had raised the blinds so he could confirm they were indeed on the Guildford road) was more conspicuous at nine in the evening than it would ever be by daylight. Then, too, there was the danger of highwaymen – not an enormous risk, true, but still a significant one.

William settled back in his seat. Whether or not Smith knew his business, there was nothing William could do about it. Once they were in France he would need his wits about him, constantly alert for the danger that Gordon was sure lurked somewhere on their route. For now, he might as well try to sleep.

That turned out to be easier said than done. While Julien and Fabrice sat tense and silent, Pascale's nervousness expressed itself in a continual commentary on the journey. Her ability to find something to talk about despite the darkness hiding the view from the window impressed William. Perhaps she did not just distribute the pamphlets. Perhaps she wrote them as well. In William's opinion the first requirement of a pamphleteer was the ability to describe the world without at any point being restricted by not knowing what you were talking about.

Provided that he didn't pay any attention to the actual words, William found the sound of Pascale's voice quite soothing. She had quite a deep voice that, despite the tension in the coach, seemed always on the verge of bursting into laughter. William closed his eyes and let the sound drift over him as the coach rocked its way steadily on into the night.

* * *

When he awoke it was already light. The air had that clarity which you seldom saw in London and he assumed that they must be near Portsmouth.

They were rattling through open country. Ironically, now that there was a view to talk about, Pascale was fast asleep, a few curls escaping from her bonnet. Julien was asleep as well, but Fabrice was sat bolt upright. William watched him from under lowered eyelids. His face showed signs of strain and they hadn't left

England yet. William wondered if he had slept at all during the night. It worried him. Fabrice had the look of a man who could not be relied on.

At least Julien, still asleep and snoring gently, carried himself like someone who might be useful in a fight – but of the three, he was the only one William felt might be able to take care of himself if they ran into trouble. It was not a reassuring thought.

Smith seemed to be sleeping silently, propped in a corner of the coach. As he turned his eyes towards him, William saw a glint of light beneath Smith's lids. Smith, it seemed, like him, was feigning sleep while assessing his unlikely gaggle of recruits.

William yawned and stretched and made a pantomime of waking up. He doubted for a moment if Smith was deceived. He wondered if the man would be travelling with them. He rather hoped he would.

They had been crossing the open Downs but now there was a village – barely a few houses. Ahead of them the road passed into some woods.

"Horn Dean," said Smith. Unlike William he had made no pretence of waking from sleep, simply opening his eyes and announcing the name of the village that was already receding behind them. "Soon be there."

The road began to run downhill and he could smell salt on the air. Suddenly he could see the sea ahead of him. The water looked as if it was covered in ships: the power and pride of Britain. He knew how much the Army in Spain relied on the Navy for supply. Without its unchallenged control of the seas, Britain could never contemplate an expeditionary campaign such as Wellington was fighting. For William, though, fresh from a campaign where he had watched his comrades starve for lack of rations, the lavish provisions of funds for sailors while his men struggled to survive in Spain – well, that rankled.

"Jealous of the Senior Service?" Smith smiled sardonically across at him.

William said nothing.

"You'll have to learn not to let your feelings show so obviously if you are going to be any good at this job."

William thought that perhaps he would as soon that Smith wasn't travelling with them after all.

Julien and Pascale were waking up now, disturbed by the conversation and the squeal of the brake as the coachman applied it to control their speed on the downhill stretch. Fabrice shook himself, trying to prepare himself for the day ahead after a night spent motionless in his seat.

Smith drew his watch from his pocket and made a show of consulting it.

"Excellent!" he said. "The *Basilisk* sails on the morning tide. We will have time to breakfast and make our *toilette*." He turned to Pascale. "Even enough time for you, my dear."

Pascale blushed. It was, William thought, becoming.

He decided he really didn't like Smith.

* * *

After the drama of their night-time drive to Portsmouth, the whole business of sailing to France seemed quite mundane. First they had made their breakfast at a quiet inn near the docks. They had, as Smith had promised, plenty of time to prepare for their voyage. William spent it half-dozing in an armchair. He reasoned that on a job like this you never knew when you would next get a decent kip. Pascale was given a room where she did whatever it was that young ladies did at a time like this, re-emerging after an hour or so, visibly more refreshed and with her errant curls firmly back under her bonnet. Julien, like William, sat back and rested while Fabrice paced to and fro until William suggested he take a walk outside.

"Best not," said Smith, and that was that. William felt, once again, like so much living cargo and he did not appreciate it. Still, he reflected, he had spent months on troop ships and this was noticeably better treatment than he had received then.

Shortly before ten Smith had led them down to the dock where a ship's boat was waiting for them. They were rowed out to where the *Basilisk* stood at anchor. There was the inevitable bustle that William always associated with a ship about to sail, but they were not allowed to watch as sailors pulled at ropes or scampered along yards. "Let's get below out of the way."

William, used to the idea that "below" on a warship all too often meant hidden way in the bowels of the vessel, was delighted to discover that they were to spend the voyage comfortably in the captain's dayroom in the stern. Smith left them there while he made his way off with some comment about checking that their baggage was safely stowed, which had had all three of William's companions rising to their feet to accompany him, but Smith had waved them firmly back. "The Navy's taking care of things now. You should relax and enjoy the voyage."

It confirmed William's opinion that Smith had served in the Navy. It didn't make him like the man any better.

* * *

The crossing was uneventful. Bells rang and sailors could be heard hurrying here and there as the watches changed. There were occasional shouted commands as sails were trimmed or headings altered. The captain came and introduced himself. He seemed pleasant enough but was clearly uncomfortable socialising with the Alien Office's agents, so he spent most of his time on deck or sequestered in his cabin.

William watched through the big stern windows as England faded into the distance. There was nothing to mark their progress – just the dull grey of the Channel churned to white by the ship's wake. At least, judging from that, they seemed to have a favourable wind.

The captain joined them for lunch – salt beef with onions – and late in the afternoon a sailor came in with cheese and biscuit and wine to wash it down with, but otherwise they were left alone. Smith had rejoined them after checking their baggage but he busied himself with papers and refused to be drawn into conversation.

William would have welcomed some more of Pascale's chatter, but as they drew nearer to France and the start of their mission even she fell silent. He thought of the evenings he had spent with men about to go into battle and the ribald chat that they would use to keep the fear at bay and he worried about the mood in the dayroom.

The atmosphere grew still more strained as the light fell. There were lamps in the cabin and Pascale suggested they might be lit, which earned her an angry glance from Julien. Smith explained. "We are in enemy waters, my dear. We can show no lights."

The *Basilisk* sailed on, ever closer to the coast of France.

* * *

It must have been almost midnight when the captain came in and whispered something to Smith.

The man from the Alien Office put away the papers he was still working on and rose to his feet.

"Madam, gentlemen: we are approaching our rendezvous. Could you please prepare to disembark."

There was a sudden rush of activity as cloaks were put on and then the realisation that there was, in fact, nothing more that they could do. They stood in the dayroom, unwilling to settle back into their seats but with nowhere to go. Julien's face was grim, but he looked like many men William had seen in the minutes before battle. He would be steady, William reckoned. Fabrice was struggling to maintain a similar expression, but failing miserably: he looked terrified. Pascale looked pale but determined.

There was a knock at the door and the bosun appeared. "Captain's compliments and could you show yourselves on deck."

Smith led them out. The stars and a sliver of moon provided enough light to make their way safely across the deck.

"It's a shame it's a new moon," Julien remarked. "We could do with being able to see our way ashore."

Smith's expression was invisible in the dark, but his voice dripped with contempt. "This night was chosen with care. Any more light and the French might well see us. And they will hear us if you continue to chatter on. I must require silence from this point."

To William there was an air of unreality about the scene. Sails were being furled as the *Basilisk* lost way, but the shouted orders that generally seemed to accompany any naval manoeuvre were absent. There was only the odd half-whispered instruction and the creaking of ropes.

The captain materialised out of the dark. "They've signalled. About half a mile ahead of our position. We'll lower the boat ready."

William had seen nothing. Away to the left he could make out the cliffs of Normandy, ghostly white under the stars – but he had seen no signal light. He turned his eyes to the sea, but saw only darkness. Major Burke should be somewhere out there. He prayed he was.

Despite the men moving silently all around him, he felt very alone.

There was the sound of rope rattling over a pulley, the bump of wood against wood and then a gentle splash as the ship's boat hit the water.

"Best get aboard now, sir." The captain spoke to Smith, carefully avoiding any acknowledgement of the agents. The Navy clearly shared the Army's feeling that confidential agents were not quite respectable.

They clambered one after another down a rope ladder into the boat that seemed to be rocking alarmingly on the waves beneath them. Pascale was wearing quite a tightly fitting dress. William was relieved that the fashion for wide skirts had passed or she would have struggled to descend with fabric blowing in all directions. As it was, she climbed nimbly down with a minimum of fuss. William was impressed. There was more to Pascale than first met the eye.

Julien swung himself down next, moving easily; then Fabrice who clung to the ladder as if fearing that at any moment a roll of the ship would throw him headlong into the water.

William followed and found himself a place among all the sailors on the boat. There seemed a lot of them and the reason became obvious as the baggage came down. First was a bundle wrapped in oilskin, not that large but obviously heavy. Pascale had to be restrained from jumping to her feet and rocking the boat as it was eased aboard. The bundle, William surmised, would be her pamphlets. It was followed by a leather case which she also watched with a proprietorial gleam in her eye, although less excitement than she had shown over the papers. William was horribly afraid that it held clothes – although he supposed that fine dresses were almost a tool of the trade for a woman spy.

Next came a box, maybe the size of the grog barrels carried on deck to serve the sailors their daily tot of rum. The care with which it was handled suggested to William that this might well be the explosive to power an infernal machine. This time it was Julien and Fabrice who watched intently as sailors reached to grab it and lay it gently on the deck.

Last came a sack that dropped with a metallic clink and then Smith followed down to join them in the boat.

They cast off from the *Basilisk* and pulled to the shore, barely a hundred yards away.

Now the cliffs were all too clear. It was difficult to estimate their height in the dark and with nothing to judge their size against, but William guessed they must be at least 150 feet high.

The boat, pulled by four burly sailors, made swift work of the journey to the shore, grounding on a narrow beach immediately below the cliff. A figure detached itself from the rock face and hurried towards them.

Smith greeted the newcomer before turning to William and the others. "This is Etienne. He will be taking charge from here on."

"Not you." Julien's tone was accusatorial.

"Good heavens, no. I'd be missed in Whitehall if I were here with you. No, Etienne is your man and an excellent guide he will be."

William looked at Etienne and liked what he saw. Unlike his aristocratic travelling companions, Etienne had the look of a sturdy peasant. He wore trousers of heavy cloth, but they had seen better days and were torn and patched. He looked to be around 40 years old with a broad face that somehow inspired confidence.

"Good! Good!" Etienne greeted each of them in turn with handshakes for the men and a kiss on the cheek for Pascale. "Come. Leave your baggage – they will take it up." He gestured to three men who were stepping from the shadows onto the beach.

Julien started to object. "I need to –" but Etienne cut him off. "Believe me, you will not be able to carry your baggage up the path. Leave it to my comrades. They have the experience and the skills."

Julien looked about to argue but Etienne just gestured ahead of him.

As he had been talking, he had been walking towards the cliff and the rest had trailed after him. Now they followed his gesture and they were close enough to see the rope that they were to climb. It stretched up out of sight.

"It's not that bad." Etienne spoke reassuringly. If you look, there are lots of footholds on the rock. Nobody is asking you to shin up the rope. You just climb up and use the rope for support."

To William's surprise, Pascale was the first to step forward. She kicked off her shoes. "Could you bring these up with the baggage?"

The stones obviously hurt her feet and she would soon be bitterly cold, but William could see why she had taken the decision she had. The boots she was wearing with her travelling clothes had quite low heels, but the leather reached well above her ankle. They were solid and supportive for walking, but climbing in them would be a nightmare.

Already she was twenty feet up, moving gracefully but with determination.

Etienne had clearly been taken by surprise and gestured to one of the young men gathering up the baggage. "Take that" – he pointed to the leather case that William thought contained a change of clothes – "and get after her. I don't want her alone up there if she loses her nerve."

There was no sign of that, though and Pascale and the man were soon lost in the darkness above them.

A while later the rope moved. Someone was signalling from above with a shake of the line rather than risk shouting down.

27

"You're next."

Julien stepped forward. He too, had taken off a pair of stout boots which he had tied together by the laces and hung around his neck. From a pocket somewhere in his cloak he had drawn a pair of dancing pumps which he was now wearing. William admired the man's forethought. His own boots were not going to make the climb easy but, then again, he had never owned a pair of dancing pumps, so he felt he had little choice when his turn came but to make the best of things.

It was a terrifying climb. Several times William's booted foot slipped and he hung from the rope, scrabbling desperately for a foothold. He concentrated on looking for any ledges or crevices that would take his weight. He only once made the mistake of looking down. He could see light on the waves far below and for a moment he was gripped by terror and hung helpless to the rope until he had gathered the courage to start climbing again.

He never knew how long he spent on that cliff. It could have been ten minutes. It could have been half an hour. All he knew was that his head was suddenly level with the ground above and strong arms were grabbing him and hauling him onto the grass.

He lay there gasping. Julien sat on the ground alongside him. Pascale, to his surprise, was standing talking animatedly to the man who had carried her case up the cliff. He made some remark that William didn't catch and she laughed that throaty laugh of hers. William was once again impressed with the pluck of the girl.

William had been lying there a while and was just beginning to sit up and try to take in his surroundings – a pointless endeavour given how dark it was – when, with much huffing and panting, Fabrice was hauled over the cliff edge to join them. Etienne followed, with (in William's opinion) an aggravating lack of any sign of breathlessness. Indeed, he gave the impression he had just been out for a short but invigorating walk.

"Come on," he said. "We can't hang around here. It's unlikely the French will patrol up here but the chasseurs sometimes take a run along the cliff tops. They do it more for exercise than in the hope of catching anyone, I think, but we'll play safe and get to cover. The others will bring your baggage."

He set off walking inland. Pascale fell into step alongside him, chatting quietly as if she was taking a stroll with friends in the country. William and Julien walked in silence, mechanically falling into step alongside each other. Fabrice followed, complaining that he was tired, his feet hurt and he needed to rest and eat. Etienne simply ignored him, which seemed to William the best thing to do.

They walked about half a mile. William couldn't see any trace of a track, but Etienne strode out confidently until William could make out a patch of deeper dark against the sky. It was a cottage – a tiny place that seemed far too small to house the whole group.

"Home sweet home," said Etienne as the door was opened and light flooded out. There was a woman waiting for them there and bread and cheese set out with flagons of cider. The woman was introduced as Marianne. ("Like that bare-titted trollop the Revolutionaries go on about – but I'm no Revolutionary, love.")

The bread was, in William's view, not as good as that which they had been given on the *Basilisk* but the cheese and cider was far superior to anything His Majesty's Navy had offered them. He realised that after his climb he was hungry and he saw the others attacking their meal with similar enthusiasm.

After his first assault on the food, William slowed and looked about him. In one corner of the room was a man who, he was sure, had not been with them on the beach. He was watching them as if weighing up how they were coping with their situation. His eyes glanced here and there and William felt that he missed very little. He certainly noticed William watching him watching them and his lips twitched into a half smile. He clapped his hands.

"Mademoiselle, gentlemen. My name is Gaston, and I will be your guide on the next stage of your journey. I am sorry to interrupt your meal, but we do have to press on. This cottage is too small for you all to be accommodated here and, in any case, I will be happier once we are further from the coast."

Fabrice, predictably, complained that he shouldn't be expected to walk any further that night but the rest put back on cloaks that they had just taken off and, with the occasional sigh, prepared to start their walk. Only Pascale thought to ask the obvious question, which was how far they were going to travel.

"Only three miles," said Gaston. "It's a short first stage. I know you must all be tired."

They started off into the night, Gaston setting a brisk pace.

Since they had landed, William had not had time to give much thought to what was happening with Major Burke, but now he began to worry. Had Burke seen the *Basilisk*? And how was he to find them in whatever safe house Gaston led them to?

CHAPTER 7: Normandy

A mile away in the darkness, Burke was asking himself the same question.

It had always been the weakest point in the plan, but it was not quite as foolish as it might have appeared. It was going to take a while for all of William's party to climb those cliffs. The lugger had made good time and he reckoned he should have arrived at Petit-Caux not that long after William was put ashore. The fight on the beach had hardly delayed him at all. He had about four miles to cover to the point where they had landed. He should arrive not that long after they climbed the cliff. Gordon's map had shown barely any houses in the area. They would have to walk from the cliff to shelter and he should be close enough to be able to hear or see something. That would be all he needed.

An hour later, stumbling in the dark over the uneven ground, he was a lot less confident. He had thought he had seen a flash of light ahead of him some time earlier, but then nothing. He had tried to walk towards it, but in the darkness and without landmarks, it was impossible to be sure that he was heading in the right direction. Then, off to his left, but nearer now, a light again. This time he was able to make out where it came from: a small cottage not that far from the cliff edge and in about the right position. The light vanished as if a door had been opened and closed again. It was enough. Burke headed in that direction.

He could hear the waves crashing against the rocks in the distance and the wind blowing off the sea. But then he heard something else: the steady rhythmic thump of footsteps.

He dropped to the ground, which not only made it harder for anybody to see him but also meant that he would more easily see people outlined against the sky. He turned to face the direction he thought the sounds were coming from and there he saw dark shapes moving across the horizon. It could only be William and the people he was travelling with. All he had to do now was to take advantage of the darkness to follow them.

He shadowed them for over an hour until they ended up at a rather splendid farmhouse. There were by now only a few hours until dawn and Burke reckoned they would travel no further that night. He would find somewhere at a safe distance to rest for the day and return in the evening to follow them again.

In this open countryside, the wind blowing in from the sea, he needed shelter. The weather was still reasonably warm, but summer was definitely over and there was a chill in the night air. It would be a pity to have got safely into France only to take a fever and die in a ditch.

He looked into the darkness for any sign of life and was rewarded by a glimpse of a light some way further inland. It was impossible to judge the distance in the dark – best, he thought, just start walking.

In the end he walked for little over a quarter of an hour. The light came from a lamp on the wall of another farmhouse, obviously a prosperous place with outbuildings clustered round a cobbled yard.

The smell of horses guided Burke towards the stables. Stables were a good place to shelter: there was often a hayloft where you could conceal yourself and the warmth from the horses below made it preferable to a cold barn.

The door at the end of the building was unlocked. Above it he could make out an opening with a pulley hoist for lifting hay bales, so there was clearly a hayloft. Easing the latch open he slipped inside.

It was quite a big stable, but most of the stalls were empty. Mangers were full and brushes and buckets were left readily to hand, but the only creatures he could make out were a couple of dray horses at the far end of the building. He wondered vaguely where the other horses were, but by now his first priority was to get some sleep. He saw a ladder that led to the loft and climbed it. It was half filled with hay bales and he wriggled his way to the back and, safely concealed, was asleep almost immediately.

After his exertions of the day before, he had expected to sleep until well after daylight, but it was still dark when something woke him.

He lay very still, listening for the sound that had disturbed his sleep.

There was the clattering of hoofs on the cobbles. He heard shouted orders and the metallic rattle of swords against their scabbards.

He had a horrible feeling he knew where the missing horses had been.

Now there were noises below as the horses were led to their stalls. There was the thump of wooden buckets as they were set on the ground and the creaking of the pump in the yard as they were filled with water.

"Get them brushed down and settled and then get to bed. We'll clean the tack after you've slept."

"Yes, sergeant."

If he had had any doubt before, it was gone now. This was a party of the chasseurs that he had been warned about on the *Mary Jane*. He had taken shelter in the enemy's stables.

"Garrigou, you're on guard. Try not to fall asleep this time."

There was some good natured jeering and then the jingle of harnesses being removed and the sound of enthusiastic brushing. Gradually the noise subsided and he heard boots crossing the courtyard as the men made their way to their quarters. Finally the last man called, "Goodnight, Garrigou. See you tomorrow," and then, except for the snuffling of the horses, there was silence.

Burke edged himself cautiously out of his hiding place and to the top of the ladder. Peering carefully down, there was no sign of Garrigou. Should he stay hidden in the hayloft and hope that nobody came up to move hay down into the

31

stables? He would probably be safe enough, but when would he be able to leave? It seemed likely that the place would be guarded until the patrol set off – and by then William's group could be on their way.

In any case, William needed to be warned. There was always a risk of French patrols, but being so close to a patrol base must escalate the risk. Perhaps that was how the network had been broken. Perhaps he had already solved the mystery of where the agents were being captured.

He dared not climb down the ladder until he knew where the guard was. If he was caught on the ladder, he was a sitting duck. Perhaps the man was outside?

Step by cautious step he headed across the loft to the opening over the stable door. Yes! There was the guard pacing back and forth in the yard.

As he watched, Burke saw Garrigou stop and take something from his pocket. He heard the scrape of flint on metal and saw a flicker of flame. The man was striking a spark from his tinderbox. Now he moved back towards the door, puffing contentedly on his pipe. That explained why he was outside the stables. With all the hay and straw, stables were notoriously prone to fires. They were not a good place to smoke a pipe especially if, as the sergeant's comment suggested, Garrigou was prone to sleeping on duty.

Garrigou had taken off his shako and placed it on the ground beside him. He stretched and yawned but remained standing. Would he eventually sleep? It was difficult to say. Burke could only hope that he would.

From where he stood, Burke could see a bald spot on the top of Garrigou's head. He wondered idly how old the man was.

Looking at that bald spot immediately below him, Burke had an idea of how he could get out of his situation.

Near the entrance to the loft, where they would have been hauled up from the yard below, were some sacks. Burke stepped carefully across to them. He guessed they held oats: it didn't really matter. He bent to lift one. It was heavy, but he could move it without dragging it, so he stepped silently back to the entrance. There stood Garrigou guarding the doorway, directly below him.

Burke lifted the sack and dropped it out of the loft.

At the last moment, something made Garrigou look up. Perhaps Burke had given an involuntary grunt as he heaved up the sack. Perhaps Garrigou had felt a movement in the air as the sack fell. It made no difference anyway. Burke saw his head tilt and a sudden look of astonishment on his face and then the sack hit him.

Burke didn't waste time climbing down the ladder. He needed to finish the man off before he had a chance to recover and raise the alarm. He jumped from the loft, landing softly, his hand already moving to the knife in his boot. One glance at Garrigou's body, though, showed him that he did not need it. The sack had struck his face, snapping his head back and breaking his neck.

Garrigou's pipe, still smoking, lay next to his body. Burke picked it up and puffed vigorously at it. He had plans for that pipe.

He dragged the body into the stables and arranged it on some hay in the first of the stalls. The horse that was there nuzzled at the body but showed no more interest in it. The horse's tack was neatly hung from pegs opposite the stall. Its saddle balanced on a rail that ran the length of the stables, ready for the horses to be tacked up when they were ridden out in the evening.

Burke walked along the stalls looking at the animals which stood quietly, sleeping on their feet. He chose one about half way along. In the poor light, there was no particular reason why this horse should be better than any of the others, but it had moved towards him as he called to it in that gentle voice that he knew would soothe a suddenly wakened animal. It had seemed happy for him to put on its tack, standing quietly as he prepared to ride out.

He had kept puffing at the pipe while he had put on the horse's harness. Now he left the animal in its stall while he walked back to Garrigou's body. He gave a final vigorous puff to the pipe until the tobacco glowed red and then he knocked it out onto the straw where the body lay.

It didn't flare up at first. He had to blow on it until a small flame started. He took a bit of burning straw and tossed it into the next stall, watching the flame flicker there.

The horses were waking now, smelling the smoke. Burke ran the length of the stables, opening the stalls.

By now the hay was well ablaze and the horses were beginning to panic, pushing their way through the door out into the yard. Leading the animal that he had selected as his own mount, Burke followed them.

Looping the reins around a tethering rail, Burke left his horse and started to ring the fire bell on the stable wall.

"Fire! Fire! Fire in the stables."

By now the yard was full of horses and within minutes they were joined by soldiers and men from the farmhouse. The horses, already panicking, were terrified as people ran for buckets and started to throw water towards the stables. Horses whinnied, pushing their way out of the yard and heading for open country. One or two of the soldiers tried to hold them back, but they had no harness to hold and some of them were beginning to rear, striking out in terror with their hooves.

In the confusion, nobody questioned Burke's presence. The soldiers assumed he was from farmhouse; those from the farmhouse assumed he was with the soldiers. He waited until the chaos was at its peak and then quietly untethered his horse, mounted and rode away.

* * *

He rode for a few miles. He hoped that in the chaos the fire would be blamed on Garrigou's smoking and there would be no immediate search for the saboteur. It was best, though, to be on the safe side. Anyway, now that he had a horse he could cover more ground.

His experience in the stables put him off the idea of spending the rest of the night holed up in an outhouse. There was, in any case, not that much of the night left. In the distance he saw, by the pre-dawn light, a small wood. Safest, he thought, to take shelter there.

He slept well, not waking until the sun was high in the sky.

As he shook himself awake, he was briefly worried that he might have missed William moving on from the farmhouse where his group was sheltering, but when he stopped to think about it, he realised this was unlikely. The group would have been exhausted and needed the rest and it was clear that their guide was anxious to move away from the coast under cover of darkness. Still, he decided, it would do no harm to keep an eye on the place.

There was no shelter within a mile of the farm. Burke was forced to ride aimlessly from one point to another, always at a brisk trot. Travellers came and went, even in this benighted part of the world. There was no reason why anyone should be suspicious of a rider passing in the distance. A rider dawdling about would be a different matter.

So the day passed. Burke grew tireder and hungrier and his horse grew tireder and hungrier too. They had ridden for hours but never moved more than a couple of miles from the farm. To top it all, it started to rain.

William must still be in the farmhouse, warm and well-fed. Burke wondered how he was getting on.

CHAPTER 8: William's journey continues

For a man used to marching with the infantry, the night's hike had been nothing at all, but William had still been pleased to rest.

He was enjoying the luxury of a real bed – and a bed with a fine stuffed mattress and blankets that showed no signs of lice or fleas. Compared with the sort of accommodation he would expect on campaign, this was paradise.

He was sharing the bed with Gaston, who snored, but that was a minor inconvenience. Fabrice and Julien had been put together in another room. They had taken their baggage in with them and William only hoped that they managed not to blow the house up overnight. Pascale had a room to herself and had announced that she intended to retire and read a novel. William wondered how their guide felt about the fact that one of his men had been carrying Pascale's book up the cliff, but nobody seemed willing to suggest that there was anything odd about this behaviour.

It was obvious that Royalist agents lived a very different life from the conditions that he and Major Burke were used to on missions. There was no doubt of Pascale's sincerity – she knew that if she was caught there was a reasonable chance that she would be put to death – but these representatives of the *ancien régime* saw no reason why they should not spy in comfort. If their present accommodation was anything to go by, the Alien Office had arranged a route that offered their aristocratic agents (Pascale was clearly an *aristo*, although William was not sure about the other two) the style of life that they were accustomed to.

When a particularly stentorian snore from Gaston finally drove William from bed, he followed the scent of hot chocolate to find Pascale already seated at breakfast attended by two servants who were piling her plate with cheeses and slices of ham. A third servant cut a baton of bread into pieces which Pascale was spreading with butter.

She smiled gaily up at him. "Come and join me. The others are all lying abed and our hosts, I believe, consider it more discreet to keep out of our way."

At the sight of the food – accompanied by jams, marmalade and honey, as well as a bowl with half a dozen different fruits – William felt suddenly hungry. A servant materialised at his side with a cup of chocolate. Would m'sieur prefer wine? William noticed a jug which he suspected (rightly) contained cider and the chocolate vanished and *cidre* appeared in its place.

He ate, half listening as Pascale recounted the details of a dream that had woken her in the night. ("And then there was a crocodile, but wearing the sweetest little bonnet.") He was relieved as Fabrice and Julien joined them. The two men seemed in good spirits, so presumably their infernal machine was in working order. William felt it was not acceptable to ask about it, so he just offered up a silent prayer thanking the Lord they had not blown up the house in the night and started on a second glass of cider.

Gaston was the last to join them, still stretching and complaining that he had hardly slept a wink. William nearly choked on his drink.

Gaston explained that they were to rest during the day. "We'll have a proper meal this evening." He looked at the breakfast on offer as if he felt personally insulted by it. "Then I'm afraid it's another night walk, but we'll be staying with a cousin of mine, so I can guarantee the food will be good."

* * *

Gaston had made it clear that no-one was to leave the house. Pascale seemed unworried by this, announcing that she still had her novel to read. Fabrice and Julien went to oversee the packing of their equipment. It was to be sent to Paris by carrier. "It's better," Gaston had explained, "that we don't risk travelling with it." It was unclear whether this was because it would be horribly incriminating or because he shared William's concerns that it might blow up at any moment. In any case it gave the two agents something to do – they fussed over their mysterious equipment like mothers fussing over an infant. Julien demanded that arrangements should be made to meet the carrier as soon as they arrived in Paris, and Gaston was forced to explain that the equipment would be stored in a safe and secret place until it was needed. No, Gaston insisted, he was not at liberty to say where: it was best for everybody that they knew no more than they had to. Julien looked so concerned at the idea of being separated from his baby that William feared he might burst into tears.

William alone had nothing to occupy him. He chafed at the confinement, looking out over the flat land that seemed to stretch forever under lowering grey clouds. He wondered where Burke was. Apart from an occasional horseman in the distance, the countryside appeared deserted. It wasn't until the fourth or fifth time he saw the distant rider that he realised it was always the same man. He allowed himself a small sigh of relief and the rest of the day seemed to pass more quickly.

That night they moved northward, paralleling the coast. The ground, that had seemed so flat when William looked out from the house, proved to conceal some steep valleys. They moved from farmland into woods, emerging eventually to the isolated half-timbered house where Gaston's cousin lived. Here, as promised, they feasted on food that was less grand than the previous night but which, in William's opinion at least, was better cooked – and nobody offered him chocolate for breakfast.

Gaston's cousin was able to provide horses for them all and the next night they were able to travel a full fifteen miles. There, at another farm, Gaston left them, passing them to the next guide, a man introduced as Marcel.

It shouldn't have mattered to William that they had changed guides. He had, after all, not known anything of Gaston when they met, any more than he knew Marcel, but the constant fear of capture by the French meant that the group had all formed a tight bond with Gaston and suddenly exchanging him for Marcel was disconcerting.

Marcel was charming – a little too charming, in William's opinion, when he was dealing with Pascale. He went out of his way to reassure everyone and promised that the next house they would be staying in would be particularly welcoming. "The Count – I don't tell you his name, but you would recognise it – his family have lived here for over 400 years. He is truly of the *ancien régime* and he has lost almost everything since the revolution. He will lay down his life for our cause."

It was a pretty speech, but the fact was that the Count had survived. What, William thought, had he offered the Revolutionaries that had meant he was allowed to live? Was this the man who was betraying the British agents?

The house that Marcel brought them to was large and must once have been splendid but it was showing definite signs of neglect. Upstairs, a couple of window panes were cracked; the woodwork needed paint. There was a large formal garden which still looked beautiful, but the rigidly geometric patterns of flowers were ragged and the grass harboured patches of moss.

The Count might not have the money that he had once possessed, but his welcome was certainly generous. It was still warm, but there was a fire in the great hall – grand still, for all that there were gaps on the walls where there had once been paintings. The Count received them himself and insisted that they sit to dinner with him. The plates were not the finest and the silverware was mismatched, but whatever other economies the Count had made, he still obviously employed a superb chef.

A delicious onion soup, creamy and flavoured with nutmeg and cloves, was followed by fish. William was not sure what the fish was but he was certain that he liked it. Then smaller dishes of salads were offered. There were radishes, figs, canapés and an anchovy salad. The main course was brought out: slow cooked lamb. The scent of the meat mixed with the smell of rosemary and thyme. William's mouth began to water.

He had just picked up his knife when there was the sound of horses arriving outside the building and fists pounding on the door.

Servants rushed in and began clearing the plates from the table while Marcel told everybody to follow him through to the kitchen.

They fled their meal, hurrying through to where the cooks were abandoning the preparation of a dessert while the lamb was being brought back from the table.

Was this the trap being sprung? Guards pouring into the house with everyone rounded up safely in the kitchen with no apparent way of escaping?

Marcel was making for the fireplace where the logs were still burning, fat dropping occasionally from the spit where the lamb had been roasted.

"Hurry!" He was gesturing them forward into the fireplace itself. Was he mad?

Only as he was standing directly in front of the flames, sweat dripping down his face, did William notice the narrow gap beyond the logs. Marcel was gesturing frantically at it and the four of them moved into the fireplace and through to a hidden room behind it.

So this was one of the Alien Office's secret rooms! William doubted, though, that the Alien Office had anything to do with its construction. Obviously the Count's family had found it useful to have a hiding place over the centuries that it had been living there.

There was no door: William assumed that a wooden door was inadvisable in a fireplace. The narrow entrance, though, was easily missed and the fire discouraged searchers. He began to think that if they were quiet they could be overlooked and would survive. That was, of course, if the Count was not part of the plot that was disrupting the line of safe houses. If he was, trapped in this windowless room with one narrow entrance they were doomed.

Marcel had lit a candle which provided a puddle of light on the side of the room away from the door. It glinted on a knife that Julien had grabbed up from the table. It would be practically useless if they were discovered, but William wished he had thought to grab another knife for himself.

Now they heard booted feet in the kitchen. Where they were hiding every word was clear.

"It's good of you, citizen, to provide such a feast. Were you expecting company?"

"Some friends had planned to come, but I think they must have been delayed on the road. I'm glad that you are here and the food will not go to waste."

It sounded as if there were just two of the newcomers.

"We'll do our best to take it off your hands. We'll eat here in the kitchen, being honest citizens and not accustomed to being waited on." There was the sound of plates being moved and the tinkle of cutlery.

"But, Count, you should join us."

"I wouldn't want to intrude." Their host's tone was stiff but polite.

"No, we insist."

There was the scraping of a chair and, after that, nothing but the sound of eating and the occasional belch.

The scent of the food drifted through to where William and the others sat listening to the intruders eating the lamb that had, only minutes earlier, been presented to them. His mouth watered. He swallowed and cursed Napoleon and all who followed him.

It can't have been more than ten minutes before there was the sound of a bench being pushed back.

"Very good, Count. It seems that the old aristos still eat well, however much they complain of hardship these days. Still, at least you are always prepared to find a crust that you will share with the local militia, eh? And we are grateful. We don't forget the men who were good to us when that Fouché sends out his orders to root out traitors. We won't put your name on the list."

There was laughter and then another voice – that of the second man who had been almost silent till now: "You aren't a traitor are you, Count?"

"I'm loyal to France."

"And to the Republic?"

"To the Republic. Of course, yes."

"Good," said the second voice. He was quieter than his companion, but his voice oozed menace. "We'll be on our way, then. For now."

The sound of their footsteps faded into the distance and the Count called from the kitchen: "They've gone. You can come out."

He looked older than he had when they sat at dinner. Marcel embraced him.

"The king will not forget what you have suffered on his account."

The Count managed a tired smile. "I only do my duty, as my family has done since the time of Louis XI. I will not abandon my family's honour lightly." Then, as the others emerged: "They have not eaten so very much. I can still offer you some of the meat and the dessert they have not touched at all."

They settled back to their food. It was at first a subdued meal, but more wine was poured and fresh fruit was added as an extra course and gradually Marcel and the Alien Office's agents relaxed. William, though, could not shake off the feeling that things could have gone very differently. If any of the men who sheltered them along the way were less honourable than the Count, it would be only too easy for one of them to buy off the militia by betraying the English spies.

This time it had been a false alarm. But how much longer would they be safe?

* * *

Despite William's misgivings, they travelled on uneventfully, moving from grand houses to farms, to the relatively humble home of a Royalist schoolmaster. Marcel gave way to another guide and he, in turn, to another and there was never any suggestion that they had been betrayed.

They had been travelling for over a week and, despite the circuitous route they were taking, William knew they were getting close to Paris. Was the whole exercise based on a false alarm? Would they arrive safe and sound in the capital? It had to be possible but his years working with Burke had taught him that when Major Burke and Colonel Gordon thought something was wrong, it was best to be cautious.

If anything was going to happen, it must be soon. They were to stay the next day at an inn. Their guide, a Royalist officer who had been dismissed Napoleon's army and now fought with the *chouan* irregulars, told them that the inn was a sort of headquarters for the resistance against Napoleon. "When we finish tonight's ride, there will be stabling for the horses. No more night riding. When you leave here you will travel into Paris like regular citizens."

39

Perhaps, William thought, it was as they travelled on from the inn that the trap was sprung. They would not all stay together. Perhaps one of the routes they used had been compromised so some were caught and others passed unmolested. That would explain why the Alien Office was unconcerned. Perhaps most agents got through and Gordon had simply been unlucky to lose so many. Or perhaps the French hadn't penetrated the network at all and Gordon's men had just been careless.

The last stage had been longer than the others and it was getting light as they emerged from woodland and their guide announced that they were almost home. Fabrice muttered something about how ridiculously long the ride had been, while Julien grunted wordlessly. Even Pascale seemed to be struggling to find something cheerful to say.

At that moment they saw a man riding towards them.

The *chouan* guide's hand went to the hilt of his sword. William cursed the fact that the rest of them were unarmed. He heard Julien swear and Pascale muttered something that might have been the start of a prayer. He turned his horse's head, ready to kick it to a gallop and make a run for it, but he was all too aware of how tired the animal was after its long ride. He could not rely on speed to make an escape.

The stranger rode closer and suddenly their guide relaxed. 'Hey, Henri!" he shouted. "You scared the life out of us."

The man – Henri, presumably, thought William – waved. "Sorry! It was such a lovely morning, I thought I'd ride and meet you on the road. I know you were planning to head straight on to ..." He left the sentence carefully unfinished. Obviously the inn they were heading to was not the only rebel household in the area.

"Thanks, Henri. You're right. I'll head off and leave my friends to your care." He turned back into the wood and vanished almost immediately while Henri looked over the four of them.

"Good! You are all here safe. We'll ride on. It's no distance."

Henri was a solidly built fellow with a face that looked somehow square, as if put together out of a cube of putty by a child with ambitions to be a sculptor but no artistic skill. He looked as if he was normally a cheerful chap – something about the lines at the corner of his mouth and the way his eyes crinkled as if always about to smile. Now, though, there was something not quite right about him.

It would have been easy to dismiss this as his imagination, but William had learned to listen to his instincts. Was there anything else to back up this vague feeling?

This was the first time on their entire journey that their guide had not taken them all the way to the place where they were to shelter. Did it matter that there had been a break in the routine? On balance, William thought it did. The Alien Office, for all its faults, had organised this until it ran like a smoothly oiled machine.

Now, just as they neared their destination, there was a sudden change in the way things were done.

William slumped in the saddle. Given how far they had ridden, it was easy for him to pretend to be more tired than he was and to fall a little behind the group.

It was a few minutes before Henri noticed but then he turned his horse to ride alongside William. "Are you alright?"

"Only a bit tired. We're almost there, aren't we?"

Henri reassured him that it was no distance.

"Don't feel you have to wait for me. I can follow on if we're that close."

No, they should all stay together. There was no hurry.

"In that case –" William made a visible effort to pull himself together. "I'll be fine." He kicked his horse on into a stumbling trot. Henri seemed satisfied and moved ahead to rejoin the others, at which point William took a deep breath and, with a silent prayer that he didn't get brained by a flying hoof, toppled from the horse.

The cry he gave as he hit the ground didn't have to be faked. Although William had become quite a good rider since his time in South America, he remained an infantryman at heart and was never entirely happy on a horse. He suspected that falling off one of the animals would be a deeply unpleasant experience and now his suspicions were proved to be all too correct.

The rest of the party stopped while Henri returned to help William to his feet. "Are you hurt?"

"No, just winded." In fact he wasn't winded at all, though he would have some interesting bruises in the morning. For Henri's benefit, though, he bent double as if gasping for breath. "Honestly, just give me a minute. I'll be fine."

The others joined them and Pascale made to dismount.

"No, ma'amselle, he does not need assistance." Henri sounded quite flustered. Again, William got the feeling that something was not quite right. His fall was a minor mishap so close to the end of their journey. Was Henri just a naturally nervous man? It seemed unlikely, given the sort of work he was doing. Why then, was he so agitated?

"It looked a nasty fall." Pascale sounded concerned. "I'd like to make sure he isn't hurt. Trust me, I've had to deal with injured men before."

It was the first time that Pascale had given any hint of the horrors that she must have lived through during the revolution and William was touched by her concern. Henri, though, again showed how rattled he was as he abruptly ordered her away. "There is no need for this. We must move on." The others seemed a little reluctant but, faced with Henri's insistence, they started to move back in the direction they had been going. Henri himself appeared torn, one moment watching them as they walked their horses away and the next moment turning to William.

"Are you sure you are alright?"

William again insisted that he would be recovered in a few minutes.

"Very well. Ride to catch us up. The path is clear enough and we will move on slowly." Then he was off, shepherding his charges towards the inn.

'Shepherding', it seemed to William, exactly described the way he was treating them: keeping them moving and trying to gather them close together. And what, he asked himself grimly, happens to the sheep after the shepherd has coaxed them to the end of the road?

As soon as Henri was out of sight, William was riding back towards the trees. Once there he pushed his horse through the undergrowth, staying far enough inside the wood to be out of sight if Henri returned.

Was he making a mistake? He wished Burke was there. The major would know what to do next.

Was Burke even in the area? He tried to think when he had last been aware of him. Yesterday he thought he might have caught a glimpse of a rider in the distance as they left the manor house where they had rested for the day. The previous night he had heard hoof beats when they had broken for a rest. On the whole, he believed that Burke was somewhere nearby, but whether the major had seen him break away from the party, let alone whether he would be able to find him in the wood, was something he was far from certain of.

He couldn't stay where he was and hope Burke would find him: he needed to take control of the situation himself. The first thing, surely, was to establish whether his suspicions of Henri were justified.

By now he had travelled far enough away from the track through the forest to feel that if he broke away from the trees he did not risk being immediately spotted by Henri. He pushed his horse out onto the open land. There was another belt of woodland ahead of him and obviously wherever Henri had been headed must be the other side of those trees. Their guide had said that they were making for an inn. An inn meant a road – certainly something bigger than the path they had been riding on. If there was a road beyond the line of trees, then all William had to do was to follow it back in the direction he had last seen his companions until he came on the inn.

It was, he thought, not a bad plan. In any case it was a plan and, until Major Burke made contact, it was the only plan he'd got.

He rode towards the trees.

* * *

It was a big road, the earth well packed down by passing traffic, although there was nothing in sight this early in the morning. William guessed that it led to Paris, probably off to the east. He squinted into the sun.

The road curved away and a rise in the ground meant he could see for only half a mile or so in that direction, but he doubted that Henri would have passed beyond where he stood and out of sight to the west in the time he had been in the wood. East it was then.

He had ridden only five minutes when he was able to see far enough round the curve to make out the roof of a building on the roadside. This, he was sure, must be the inn.

He left the road and headed across the higher ground that meant he would be invisible from the building. If all was well he would ride in and apologise for getting lost, but if not…

What would he do if not? There had been no sign of any other rider. If Major Burke was in the vicinity, he was lying low.

William thought of all the times he had scouted out the land for Burke. He would think of this as just another scouting expedition. Once he was in a position to make his report, then would be a good time to worry about who to make it to.

There were no trees on this side of the road and nothing to tether his horse to. He let the reins trail and dropped the biggest rock he could see on them. The horse, he reckoned, was too tired to make any serious attempt to run off.

Dropping to the ground, he crawled cautiously to the top of the rise and peered over at the inn.

There was no sign of life.

Perhaps everyone was safe inside except for Henri who was out looking for him. If that was the case, then eventually the guide would return. At that point, William decided, he would show himself. Until then, he would wait.

He had no watch, but he guessed half an hour must have passed when he saw a horse travelling towards the inn from the other side of the road. As it drew nearer he saw that the rider was Henri. So the guide had left everyone in the inn and gone back to look for him. He had been suspicious for no good reason.

He was about to rise to his feet and wave down at Henri when a hand fell heavily on his shoulder and pushed him back to the ground.

"We'll give it a few more minutes I think, sergeant."

He rolled onto his back and looked into the grimly smiling face of Major Burke.

"I've never been so glad to see you, sir. And if you ever give me a shock like that again, I won't be responsible for my actions."

CHAPTER 9: An inn near Paris

For most of last week Burke had wished he could change places with William. While William moved from comfortable house to comfortable house, he had not slept in a proper bed since he had left London. He could hardly turn up at an inn at daybreak and ask for a room until that evening. It would be as good as an admission that he was up to no good and, in a country where Napoleon's secret police were everywhere, he could not expect his journey to escape the attention of the authorities.

Every morning he would scour the area around whatever house the Alien Office was using to shelter its agents, hoping ideally for a barn but happy to accept any ruin that might offer shelter during the day. The Alien Office, though, had carefully chosen isolated houses for refuge and most days there was nothing. This meant, too, no chance of finding anywhere to eat. On his second day following William he had ridden a mile to an isolated farm where he had claimed to be a traveller who had started out before breakfast and he offered good money for bread and cheese. The farmer was obliging and even offered (for an exorbitant price) some ham. Burke had enthused over the food and persuaded the farmer (for an even more outrageous sum) to sell him cheese and ham for the road.

He had sheltered one night in an orchard, which meant as many apples as he could eat, but he had spent most of his time hungry. He watched enviously as his horse grazed on whatever grass it could find of an evening and he dreamed of steak and over-cooked vegetables.

By now, he was ravenous, tired and increasingly convinced that they were on a wild goose chase. They had almost reached Paris and all seemed well.

He had held back well behind William and his friends as they rode through the wood. The track was clear enough even in the dark and he didn't want to risk being heard.

He had not been close enough to hear Henri's arrival, but the regular sound of hoof beats ahead of him had stopped. A few minutes later he heard a single horse coming towards him. He pushed off the track and watched as the guide who had led William this far rode back the way he had come. The man rode easily and, as far as Burke could tell through the screen of trees, was quite relaxed. It seemed there was no problem with the arrangements so far.

Burke moved back onto the track and headed forward. Just then he heard William cry out. Was this the ambush he had been waiting for? It seemed unlikely. Why take the group in the wood instead of waiting until they were in a house where they would have little chance of escape? Burke pulled his horse up and sat motionless, listening. There were no screams, no curt commands to surrender.

He heard the group moving away and cautiously started to follow. A minute or two later, he stopped at the sound of a single horse pushing through the trees.

If the party had split up, the only thing that made any sense was that William had broken away for some reason. If so, he clearly wasn't in any immediate danger. Burke followed carefully after the rest of the group.

He had to fall back as the wood gave way to open ground, but he had no problems working out where they were heading. Only a few minutes after leaving the woods he saw a large inn ahead of him. He got off his horse to make himself less obvious against the horizon and stood watching as the four riders dismounted in a cobbled yard at the back of the inn. Two grooms came out to take the horses and lead them to stables that fronted onto the yard.

There was something about the grooms that did not sit well with Burke. As far as men of their class went, grooms had a certain amount of respect. They were in charge of valuable animals and could hold their jobs only if they were trusted to care for them well. This gave them a relaxed air that some men would construe as arrogance. It was reflected in the way they moved – with the natural grace of those who spent most of their lives with animals and who were at home with them. These grooms, though, moved rigidly, holding themselves artificially erect and stiff.

Burke knew that look.

"Soldiers or I'm a Dutchman."

At least, he thought, they now knew how far Fouché had got with penetrating the network. The good news was that he had not got far. The better news was that William had escaped the trap, but that left three of the Alien Office's agents prisoners of the French. Burke's orders had not specifically mentioned rescuing the agents, but he knew that Gordon would expect him to do his very best.

The gendarmes, Burke knew, generally operated in units of six. It was reasonable to assume that there were six there. Mounting a rescue, even if he found Sgt Brown to help him, was not a serious prospect. The gendarmes were elite troops and he and Brown had one knife between them.

The first thing to do was to find Brown. Even unarmed, two people were going to be more useful than one.

He looked behind him at the forest. He had heard Brown's horse crashing through the woods to the west. He couldn't believe that his sergeant would have left his companions to their fate, so it seemed most likely that he had carried on in that direction until he was a safe distance away and then circled round to the inn.

Burke looked at the terrain. A road ran left to right across his view and beyond that the land rose slightly. He nodded to himself. Anyone who had fought with Wellington would recognise the usefulness of the dead ground just the other side of the ridge. That's where his man would be.

Burke had the advantage that he didn't have to hide in the wood. Nobody would be out looking for him. He kicked his horse on and cantered across the open ground until he was half a mile or so from the inn, crossed the road and started back on the other side of the ridge. Sgt Brown was exactly where he had expected him to be.

He could not resist showing off the skills he had perfected in guerrilla campaigns in Egypt, South America and Spain. Slipping off his horse he moved silently forward.

CHAPTER 10: Together again

"You really need to protect your rear, Brown."

William made an obscene remark, which Burke pretended not to hear.

"You're sure it's a trap, sir?"

"Absolutely sure. Wait and see."

They had waited an hour and Burke was beginning to wonder if he had misread the situation, when a cloud of dust in the direction of Paris suggested a coach approaching at speed.

"Ah!" said Burke. "They decided to call for transport only when the trap had closed. A wise decision even if it has delayed moving the prisoners."

The coach drew up opposite where Burke and Brown lay hidden. The doors of the inn opened and William's erstwhile companions emerged, their hands tied behind their backs. They were escorted by two splendidly uniformed men of the gendarmerie. The prisoners were pushed, none too gently, into the coach and were followed by their guards. Two more gendarmes (Burke thought he recognised the grooms) appeared on horseback and the coach and its escort turned and started back towards Paris.

"That's awkward."

"We've got to do something, sir." William would not admit to any special fondness for Pascale, but the idea of her in the hands of Napoleon's soldiery upset him.

"We shall make every effort, William. First, though, we need to establish where the prisoners are being taken. Unless you can whistle up half a dozen armed Royalists, we have no chance of saving them on the road. Our best chance is to break them out of durance vile wherever they are to be held."

William grunted an acknowledgement of the truth of this remark. He knew that the English had an excellent track record when it came to springing spies from French gaols. Why the French made their prisons so easy to escape from was a mystery to him. He put it down to the revolutionary temperament: after all, if you spent your whole time talking about *Liberté* it stood to reason, he thought, that you weren't going to put your heart into building prisons.

They mounted and set off along the road, following the coach.

"I think we need to separate again I'm afraid, William. Follow the dust of the coach but stay out of sight. I'll turn back for you when I can. If all else fails we'll find each other at the site of the old Bastille. I imagine that's a popular meeting place."

Before William could object, Burke was gone, galloping after the coach.

Once it came in sight he slowed to a rapid trot – fast enough to catch up with them but not so fast as to suggest an extended pursuit.

The gendarmes looked at him suspiciously, but he gave his most disarming smile and pulled alongside one of the outriders.

"I'm glad to see you."

The gendarme stared at him but said nothing.

"I'd heard there were sometimes brigands on the road out here and I was worried riding it alone."

"There's no brigands here." The man spoke curtly. "Not while the gendarmerie are keeping it safe."

"Oh, yes, absolutely. The gendarmerie do an excellent job. But you can't be everywhere, can you?"

The gendarme gave him a hard stare. "We're here now, aren't we?"

"*Absolument!* And that's why I feel safe riding with you. You are going to Paris?"

"We are."

"Whereabouts in Paris?"

"What concern is that of yours, citizen?"

"I'm travelling to Montmartre. I was wondering if you were going in that direction."

"No, citizen. We are heading for Île de la Cité. But don't worry." He looked disdainfully at Burke. "Even a little pipsqueak like you will be safe enough once we're in town."

Burke thanked him profusely and fell in behind the carriage. It meant getting covered in dust, but the alternative was to be on the receiving end of the gendarme's contempt for the rest of his journey and, on the whole, he preferred to get dusty. He had, in any case, learned all he needed to know. There were many prisons in Paris but only one on Île de la Cité: the Conciergerie.

* * *

As soon as they reached the capital, Burke left the gendarmes and headed towards Montmartre. Once the carriage was safely out of sight, though, he turned back and rode the way they had come until he saw William stretching his legs on a bench outside a tavern a couple of miles down the road.

"Comfortable, are you?"

William grinned. "I thought you'd appreciate the chance to sit down and drink at your ease. I know you haven't been enjoying the food that we've been treated with, so I've ordered for you. Should be out in a few minutes."

Burke sketched the sign of the cross. "Bless you, my son. All your sins are forgiven you." He sat down alongside William, who had already poured a glass of wine for him. "I see you're sticking to the cider."

William took a swig. "It's good stuff. And you want me to blend in."

"Indeed." In the interests of blending in, both were speaking French. Burke was relieved to hear William's French was much improved and was about to tell him so when the patron emerged from the tavern to place a plate of lamb stew in front of him. The smell reminded him of how long it was since he had sat down to a hot meal and for a while there was no further conversation while he concentrated on his food.

He had finished the stew, mopping the last few drops with the remains of the bread that had followed it onto the table, and then he had demolished a wedge of cheese and an apple. William – no slouch himself when it came to putting food away – watched in awe, but eventually Burke licked his lips and claimed to be satisfied.

"So where to now, sir?"

"I think it's time you saw something of Paris, young William. So we're going to visit the town and then see if we can get ourselves into gaol – though preferably in a way that lets us get out again."

CHAPTER 11: Île de la Cité

James Burke and William Brown lounged on the south bank of the Seine looking across the river at the lowering bulk of the Conciergerie. There had been a castle on this site for centuries and although it was no longer a military fortification the high walls and towers were far from welcoming.

"How do you get in?"

Burke gave Williams question some thought. "There doesn't seem to be a watergate. I suppose the entrance must be on the land side."

There was a silence while the two men sucked their teeth and considered the possibilities. Where they were, with the river between them and the old fortress, nobody would suspect them of taking an unhealthy interest in the place, but they were worried about getting too close. Burke looked at the bridge that ran across the Seine. It was busy with carts and pedestrians crossing to and fro.

"It doesn't look as if there's anything to stop people just wandering past. We might as well take a closer look. We're not going to be able to get anyone out from over here."

William grunted something that might reasonably have been taken for assent and they set off across the bridge.

The place did not look any more salubrious as they got closer. It seemed to have been thrown together from bits of different buildings. Three round towers with conical roofs screamed 'fortress' and the walls near them looked as if they could withstand quite a bit of punishment if anyone tried to storm them. Nearer the bridge, though, was a variety of different styles, all with regular windows that Burke thought the famous Paris mob could have broken into with no problem at all. Come to think of it, he recalled something about the mob seizing control of the building and he knew that it was there that the unfortunate Queen Marie Antoinette had stood trial for her life. He had always assumed that the trial must have been held amid some sort of pageantry and splendour, but there was little sign of that.

The corner of the building was a great square tower. The bell at the top suggested decoration rather than defence, as did the large glazed windows on the lower floors. The whole effect reminded him rather of civic halls he had seen in Belgium, where grandiose clock towers seemed favoured in towns with no other claim to fame

It was almost noon and they had nearly reached the tower when the noise of chiming drew Burke's eye up to a huge clock, apparently of some antiquity, that faced out over the road that led from the bridge. Again, Burke was left with the impression of a provincial town-hall.

Now he could see the entrance: an open gate led into a courtyard from which a short flight of steps ran up to the main door. There was a steady stream of men going in and out of the building, many of them in the black gowns of lawyers and others looking like clerks. There were guards at the door and, while most people passed unchallenged, even as James and William dawdled their way past they saw someone stopped and turned firmly back.

"We'd better not hang about here too long. Those guards have eyes in their heads and I don't want them noticing us. If they can pick out strangers in that crowd, then they have a remarkable memory for faces."

They carried on along the street. From this side they could see the roof of what Burke imagined must be a grand hall – bigger by far than anything he had seen in England. Away from the main building, but clearly part of the same complex, soared the spire of a church. The roof of the building could just be made out over the cluster of offices that fronted onto the street. It looked as if it was on a scale to match the grand hall. From here it was much easier to see it as the royal palace it must once have been.

They moved on to the next street without learning anything more.

"Do you think you could manage another drink, William?"

William, it seemed, could.

He was not pleased to discover that the sophisticated taverns of Paris did not offer the *cidre* he had enjoyed on his journey from the coast, but James and he shared a bottle of red wine and he had to admit that it wasn't at all bad. James realised, to his surprise, that he was already hungry again and the wine was soon joined on the table with bread and cheese and ham and the two of them sat in silence for a while enjoying their meal.

Once they were no longer hungry or thirsty, Burke outlined the problem. They knew nothing about the Conciergerie and without some notion of what went on there – because it was obviously much more than just a prison – they weren't in any position to help the agents languishing somewhere inside.

Burke looked down at his clothes, soiled by a week of travelling and living rough.

"I think it's time I saw my tailor."

"Your tailor?"

"Yes. I need to get myself a new outfit of smart city clothes: the latest thing in Paris fashion."

"Can I ask why, sir?"

"Well, William, it seems to me that we need new friends and what better place to make new friends than at a party. So I'm going to get myself some fancy clothes and hit the town."

William nodded. "It's a plan, I suppose. Do I get new clothes?"

Burke looked him up and down. "No," he said. "Your clothes are good enough for a servant."

"I don't get to go to the party, then."

Burke laughed. "No, William. You don't." And then, responding to the expression on his sergeant's face: "I think Colonel Gordon's funds will run to enough for you to buy a few drinks while you make some new friends of your own. Anything you find out could be useful."

He was rewarded with a broad smile. "An evening of drinking for our country it is, sir. And I'll wager my evening will be more fun than yours."

"Let us hope, Brown, that both our evenings are fun. And," he added, "productive."

* * *

Col Gordon was often a harsh master but, Burke thought, generous in the provision he made for his men in the field. Knowing that Burke would have to travel light but that he could well need a different wardrobe once he had made it to Paris, the colonel had provided him with a generous quantity of gold to buy anything he might need. He had even given him the address of a tailor he could recommend.

Burke judged that about half an hour had passed since they had been deafened by the Conciergerie clock's noon chimes. William's companions must have been in the prison for several hours. He needed to get started and he could do nothing without new clothes. Over the years he had discovered that it was remarkable what people would tell you provided you looked respectable enough. And, almost as remarkable, how unwilling they might be to talk to you if you did not look the part. He hoped that Gordon's tailor was a fast worker and that the British Army had provided him with sufficient funds to encourage him to put any other work aside until Burke was properly turned out.

* * *

In the distance the clock could be heard striking the hour as Burke sauntered into the tailor's shop. The tailor was not sat at his work and Burke suspected he was about to take a break for lunch. Indeed, the man glanced at him as he entered and seemed about to wave him away when he paused as if uncertain how best to deal with this new customer. Burke had some sympathy with him. His clothes had never been the latest in urban fashion in the first place and they were now distinctly shabby but his manner was that of a fashionable man about town. Burke could not say how he did it himself, but he could, when necessary, almost instinctively adopt this persona. It was something about confidence in his walk, the way he held his head, the faintly haughty yet sympathetic expression on his face.

As the tailor hesitated, Burke began to speak and his smoothly upper-class Parisian accent had the required effect. The tailor put aside his doubts about Burke's clothing and concentrated on what his new customer was asking for.

"The thing is, citizen …" Burke was careful to address the tailor correctly. It was one thing to appear upper-class, but another to identify too closely with the *ancien régime*. "The thing is that I was the victim of an --" He paused. "An accident on the road into town." The tailor gave an understanding nod.

"Such 'accidents' m'sieur have been all too common of late."

Burke gave a resigned Gallic shrug. He thought of the arrogant gendarmes that morning: so much for stopping highway theft.

"Alas my baggage was lost in the 'accident' and my clothes appear to be the worse for the encounter. Fortunately my funds were concealed about my person." He held up a purse which he had filled with coins that had, indeed, been concealed in his clothing and in the hollow heels of his boots. It clinked in a manner that the tailor seemed to find quite satisfactorily.

"The problem is that I am engaged to dine in society this evening and it is imperative that I am properly dressed for the occasion."

"This evening, m'sieur? I regret ..." (and he really did sound regretful) "I regret that that will be quite impossible."

"Really," drawled Burke, sounding entirely unconvinced. "Even if I pay you double?"

"Double!"

Burke could see the tailor struggling. After so many years of war, Burke knew that money must be tight, even as Napoleon reaped the rewards of his defeat of Austria. But to produce an entire outfit by evening was, he knew, a challenge for even the fastest of workers.

"I will be happy if my man can collect it at, say, ten."

Nine hours! Burke could almost read the tailor's mind. No lunch, no dinner. Perhaps he had something he was making for another customer that he could adapt to fit Burke. James saw his eyes running over his figure, assessing it. Yes, that was it: the man thought he had something that might be made to fit. But still the tailor hesitated.

Burke drew a gold louis from the purse. "Perhaps a little something on account."

The sight of ready money proved the turning point. The tailor produced a cord and Burke was measured with particular care, for there would obviously be no time for a second fitting. A knot here marked the distance from wrist to elbow, another there from elbow to shoulder. Would the gentleman be wearing trousers? Burke certainly would. Revolutionary Paris was hardly the place for breeches and he would not need a wig either. Could the tailor recommend a hatter?

More cord was produced to measure Burke's legs. Yes, the tailor could recommend a hatter. A cousin, quite nearby. And, though these are very good boots for the country, maybe the gentleman would like a recommendation as to where he could buy footwear for town?

Burke was spending Gordon's money like water. He might as well, he decided, spend it with the tailor's family. Yes, he agreed, he would like some more boots.

The tailor was, by now, humming happily as he finished measuring up. Burke thought that if he sounded so happy despite the prospect of more than eight hours of frantic cutting and sewing, then he was undoubtedly on a generous commission from his cousins. Still, he did need the clothes and anything that might help get the Alien Office's agents out before they gave up their secrets to Fouché's interrogators had to be worth a few more louis.

"My man – " Burke gestured toward William who had waited like the perfect servant, almost invisible in the background. "My man will collect it at ten."

CHAPTER 12: A night out in Paris

Like Burke, William had been the beneficiary of Gordon's special fund. In fact, as he was travelling in a group with baggage he had carried the majority of their money. Between them they had more than enough to see them comfortably through their first days in Paris and Burke decided that now his immediate dress needs had been dealt with the next thing was to find a good hotel and spend a few hours on a comfortable bed. It wasn't as if he could do anything else until he could appear in public respectably dressed.

They found a place in the centre of town, nor far from the Conciergerie and even closer to Napoleon's palace at the Tuileries. Burke enjoyed the idea of spying on the French Emperor from under his nose.

Ensconced in a luxurious room in a fashionable hotel (Gordon was paying after all) Burke was conscious that his clothes were not only shabby but, after a week of living rough, there was an odour that did not fit with the image that he intended to cultivate. He ordered a bath and a train of servants arrived in his room, bearing a bathtub, buckets of water – both hot and cold – towels and soap. They seemed to expect him to bathe while they stood around to watch. He could only assume that to the average Frenchman a bath was an arcane ritual that they would watch with attention and tell their families about when they returned home at the end of the day. Burke, though, denied them that pleasure, shooing them all out except for a chambermaid who poured the water and arranged the towels. She was pretty, if plump, and her manner clearly suggested that she would happily have remained to help James wash and offer any other scrvices he might have in mind. He was tempted, but he was tired and had to be at his best that evening. He thanked her and saw her off with a generous tip before allowing himself to soak until the water began to cool. Then he wrapped himself in a towel, threw himself on the bed and was almost immediately asleep. William, who was back to playing the role of Burke's servant, was somewhere up in the attic and could be relied on to collect the clothes and wake his master in the evening.

He awoke refreshed to find William laying out shirt, trousers and coat.

"He's done a decent job," was William's opinion and Burke was inclined to agree with him. The shirt was a little long in the sleeves, but nothing that would draw attention. The coat showed some signs that the seams had been stitched in a hurry. Burke had suspected that the tailor had taken in a coat that he had been making for someone a little less slim than him and the hasty stitching of the seams suggested to him that he had been right.

"I got you a cravat too. You'd forgotten it." William sniffed with the disdain of a real valet. But, like the ideal gentleman's gentleman that he was pretending to be, his choice was, in Burke's opinion, excellent.

He dressed quickly. He had bought a pair of dancing pumps as well as the boots. The boots were more practical, but hardly party wear, so pumps it was.

He admired himself in the mirror. "What do you think, William? Shall I not be the cynosure of any party I attend tonight?"

William sniffed. "It's hardly Saville Row, is it?"

"Perhaps not, William, but it's maybe for the best. The idea is to blend in, after all."

And blend in he did. With his blue tail-coat and a bicorn hat – the popularity of which must surely have owed something to Napoleon – he was as respectable a Parisian gentleman as he could have wished.

It was close on eleven as he left the hotel, William accompanying him.

He should, by rights, travel to an evening's entertainment in a carriage but, leaving aside the fact that he did not have a carriage (one could, after all, be hired), he had no idea where his party was. His plan, which he admitted to himself was on the vague side – but still a plan – was to walk the fashionable district until the presence of a line of carriages showed him where the best parties were to be found.

In the event he found a procession of carriages fighting their way through a passage off the Rue St Honoré less than 20 minutes from the hotel. Following them, he found himself in a cobbled courtyard where the carriages were trying to find space to put themselves, having dropped their elegant guests at the porte-cochere in front of what appeared to be the grandest of several apartments sharing the yard. The guests passed a couple of liveried footmen who glanced at their invitations as they entered the house.

William sniffed. "It's a shame you haven't got your invitation isn't it?"

"Alright, William: time to put on a show."

William, still in his travelling clothes, seemed somehow to shrink. Where, a moment before, there had been a servant, scruffy but unspectacular, there was now an aggressively hulking villain. He lurched towards the door, shouting drunken abuse as he drew nearer. One of the footmen left his post to shoo him away, but suddenly William was holding a cosh in his hand. ("I'd feel better with a knife," he had complained, but Burke had insisted that they avoid bloodshed.) The footman hesitated and his companion abandoned his post to provide support.

The next coach in line had pulled up and the guests were huddled under the porte-cochere, watching the excitement. Burke simply joined them. He counted silently to ten and then, speaking loudly, but not shouting, called out, "I say, this looks a bit unpleasant. Hadn't we better get the ladies inside?" Both the gentlemen in the party nodded and ushered the ladies past the now unguarded doors with much twittering and grasping of fans. Burke simply followed them in, confident that

William was now moving rapidly towards the gate and that the footmen would be reluctant to follow him.

Ahead a marble staircase led up towards the sounds of conversation. Under the hub-bub he could faintly hear music. There was much clinking of glassware – always, he felt, a good sign at a party.

A flunky materialised beside him. Would he care to leave his hat? The flunky departed, carrying away his hat and leaving him with a small wooden token. In the best households, he knew, the flunky would simply remember him and have the hat ready as he left. He was quite glad this was not such a household. If it were, there was always a danger that someone working there would realise he had not been invited.

Beyond the landing was a ballroom where, though it was still early, the party was already warming up. The men, like him, wore tail coats in a variety of more or less drab colours – blues and russets predominating. There were, of course, some gorgeously apparelled military men, generally wearing the peacock blue of the French army with much gold braid and occasional flashes of scarlet. The principal colour, though, was yellow. It was clearly the fashionable colour of the year and there were hardly any of the ladies there who weren't wearing it. Not that, in many cases, they were wearing a lot of anything. Burke considered himself a broad-minded man of the world, but he had visited many a bordello where the women exposed less flesh than was on exhibition here. The French, he knew, had a reputation for licentiousness, but he was surprised to find it so publicly on display. Many of the women wore silks so fine that they were practically transparent and a few had their bodices cut so low that their nipples were exposed. All, though, had white gloves, often running up beyond the elbow, almost as if the ladies of the city had decided to declare the forearm an erogenous zone.

A waiter passed with a tray of champagne glasses and Burke helped himself to one. The party hadn't really got going. Men were still gathered in groups exchanging small talk. The dancefloor was virtually deserted and although women were looking around with eyes that sparkled with mischief, no mischief was actually taking place yet.

A group of men in respectable – and, Burke thought, rather dull – coats were standing uncertainly just inside the doors. They had the air of people who were not quite sure that they belonged. Burke suspected that they would be unlikely to hold any secrets about the Conciergerie or anything else, but they could at least give him some useful background about the place.

He introduced himself as a stranger in town, adopting the aura of a provincial still excited by the idea that he was here in the capital of Europe's new Empire. Where should he be going? What sights should he see?

There was little a Parisian enjoyed more than condescending to somebody born with the crippling disadvantage of not being a child of the capital. He must visit the new restaurants that were springing up all over the place – so much better than anything he would be used to. And the gardens: "The Emperor still keeps the

Tuileries Gardens open for people to stroll in and enjoy. He may wear a crown these days, but he still cares about the common man." Napoleon's recent victories in Austria had brought prosperity to the capital and Napoleon's star still shone brightly there, however many émigré dissidents the British were smuggling in.

"Can you visit the Tuileries?" Burke asked innocently. The question provoked some mirth. It was the Emperor's home; it was his office; it was a centre for government. It wasn't a place for random strangers to explore. What about the Louvre? Oh, the Louvre was quite different. It wasn't a palace any more. It was a museum – the *Musée Napoléon* – a celebration of arts and antiquities from across the French Empire. It sounded to Burke like a repository of plunder and loot, but he looked appropriately impressed and promised to make sure to visit it.

"What about that building I was admiring across the Seine – the one with the remarkable clock tower?"

"You mean the Conciergerie." The speaker was a younger man whose tone suggested that old buildings were far too boring to be worth attention. "Yes, that used to be a royal residence too, but now it's offices and courts. There's an old church there where they store state records and a few prison cells. It's not open to the public, not that there's anything you'd want to see there."

A man with grey hair and a coat that may have seen better days leaned forward. "It was the main prison during the Terror, you know. Filled with poor wretches crammed into the passages. Hauled up into court, sentenced in the morning, executed in the afternoon."

The others in the group edged away. Clearly it was considered bad form to talk about those days. Burke found himself alone with the old man. "But the other fellow said there were only a few cells."

"Now, yes. Everything is very tidy under our new ruler. The Conciergerie has been tidied up. But it's not a place I'd want to visit."

Burke put an appropriately curious look in his face. The old man leaned still closer. "One of those towers by the river," he said. "They call it the *Tour Bonbec*." The man paused dramatically. The Tower of the Good Beak – as you might speak of a bird with its beak open to sing. Burke couldn't immediately see any reason for the dramatic pause, but then it came to him just as the old man spoke again. "The tower where the little birds all sing. It's where they kept the torture chamber."

* * *

The party was beginning to warm up. Groups of men sauntered up the grand staircase with an arrogant confidence that matched their clothes – all in the latest styles and so new Burke almost expected to spot tailor's chalk at the seams. Burke saw the group he had been talking to cast nervous glances towards the newcomers and then, as if retreating before a superior army, start to edge their way out.

The newcomers, Burke decided, were the children of the rich: those who somehow seemed to glide effortlessly into positions of power after every revolution, even though they were so often exactly those who the revolution had been supposed to topple.

A man with dark curly hair looked over toward Burke, a quick glance assessing his clothes, his manner and the knot of his cravat. The tailor had obviously done a good job in the few hours available to him because the young man detached himself from the group he had arrived with and crossed the room towards him.

"I haven't seen you at one of M Rabault's parties before."

"No," Burke admitted. "I'm new in Paris."

"What brings you here?"

"Here Paris, or here the party?"

"Well the party must be the wine and the beautiful women. Perhaps Paris is the same?"

Burke laughed politely and then started his story. These newcomers would be uninterested in impressing some provincial parvenu. Burke slipped easily into his new persona. He was a refugee from Ireland, escaping the iniquities of English rule. He had some land in Ireland and the money was still reaching him through a network of friends, but he was thinking of setting up in business in France. What sort of business? Buying, selling, the movement of goods across borders.

And so Burke – or de Burgh as he introduced himself – met several gentlemen who were all, they said, sure that they knew of opportunities for a man who was resourceful and knew how to sail with the tide. Visiting cards were slipped into his hand. Alas! he had no cards to give them, being but newly arrived in town. It was true, of course, but it also suited Burke for it to be easier to find these men than for them – or anyone else – to find him.

He was just discussing the increasingly uncomfortable position of the British troops in Walcheren and the business possibilities that would be opened up once the island was re-taken by the French ("They'll need food in the short term and looms and suchlike as they rebuild the weaving sheds") when they were interrupted by two young women.

"We have come for a party and all we see is you men clustering around and talking business," complained the younger of the two.

"You all fuss over this man," said her friend, gesturing towards Burke and then, to him: "You have not been here before, I think."

"No, this is my first time."

"You are not from Paris, monsieur. Perhaps not even from France. I can tell by your accent."

Burke could speak flawless French from his years with the Regiment of Dillon, but he had taken care to let a bit of an accent slip through.

"You are most perceptive, ma'amselle. I am from Ireland."

"How romantic." She had brown hair worn short in what was clearly the fashion. The mass of curls looked to Burke's eye not entirely natural, but her smile seemed unforced and a sparkle in her brown eyes suggested the possibility of an interesting evening. He could not, in any case, carry on any more business talk. The room had been getting steadily busier and it was time to dance, not to bore the ladies by dragging their partners away to talk of money and contracts.

"Do the Irish dance? I have heard that they – what is the word – 'jig'."

"I've heard it said," he replied gravely, "but I must confess I have never seen it done."

She laughed – she had a pretty laugh – and he offered his arm. She slipped her respectably gloved arm into his and pressing slightly closer to him than was strictly necessary, moved with him towards the centre of the room where space had been cleared for a dance floor.

The orchestra had been reinforced since earlier in the evening and a dozen or so musicians made a brave show at making themselves heard above the din of conversation. Burke had heard better, but they kept time well enough and the girl – her name, he had learned, was Amelie – was a good dancer. She was tall and her cheek, in those dances where they held each other, came close to his. Gavotte followed quadrille followed cotillion and Amelie showed no sign of wanting to find another partner. The room became hotter and Amelie's face began to flush.

"Would you care to take some air?"

She agreed that some fresh air would be good and they went out through the doors at the other side of the ballroom that led out onto an outside landing: a stone balcony from which steps ran from right and left to a garden below. Burke was impressed. A garden, even a small one – and, in truth, this was little more than a courtyard with a few bushes – was a luxury here in the heart of Paris. In the shadows below them they could hear giggling.

Amelie's dress, by the standards of the company, offered generous protection from the chill but, even so, she shrugged the fabric to cover more of her chest. "They must be maddened by desire to face the cold for a few minutes of privacy."

Burke smiled. He had his mission to think of: he had no intention of seducing this young woman.

"Of course," Amelie went on, "it may be that they have no choice. Not many will have their own apartment conveniently to hand."

That, Burke agreed, was unlikely to be the case.

Amelie smiled. "How convenient, then, that I do."

She laughed and James was conscious that his astonishment must have shown on his face. Fortunately she was not offended. She was, it turned out, one of the many ladies who waited on Napoleon's wife, Josephine.

"We are not 'ladies in waiting' like with your Prince Regent." She laughed again. "For one thing we are not obliged to give ourselves to the Emperor, although –" and there was a coy fluttering of eyelashes – "it's not unknown." And she laughed again. "Josephine does not like it, though," she added matter-of-factly.

"Anyway, as I am not officially part of the great man's court, I don't get an apartment in the Tuileries. But obviously, I do have to live nearby. Would you like to see it?"

Suddenly, his mission did not seem as all-consuming as it had a few minutes earlier. It was not as if he could advance the release of the prisoners before the next day in any case.

CHAPTER 13: *La Tour Bonbec* – the first night

It was past midnight. The corridors of the Conciergerie were almost deserted. Fouché finished his daily report for the Emperor and stretched. He was tired but it was too soon to be making his way home. It had taken weeks to trace the path of the English agents back from 'The Sign of the Doves' to the inn outside Paris. Now they had three more prisoners and he could start to work back along the chain of safe houses that the English used.

"Le Blanc!"

One of his men hurried from the outer office.

"Have the woman taken to the *Bonbec*. I'll start with her."

He set off to walk to the old torture chamber. Not that any torture was to be expected – not there, at any rate. In the *Tour Bonbec* he would start with a civilised discussion, just as he had with that girl Sofie from 'The Sign of the Doves'. Sofie had been allowed to go with no harm done to her at all. Fouché hoped it would be the same with this woman. 'Pascale' she called herself. He doubted it was her real name. He doubted she was an innocent like Sofie, but he hoped she was. He revered women. It was, he supposed, one of the superstitions he had inevitably acquired when he was being educated by the priests of the Oratorians. He didn't like to see them hurt, though he gave the orders when he had to. His old religious superstitions could not be allowed to get in the way of his duty to the State.

He walked slowly to the tower and limped up the stairs to the room where he would conduct the interrogation. This girl – this 'Pascale' – would have had further to travel, but he knew she would already be there when he arrived. He was tired and the limp from his club foot was always worse when he was tired – especially on the spiral stairs of the tower.

She was sitting in front of the table. It seemed a courtesy to have her seated but, in fact, he did it simply so that she would have to look up at him when he entered the room. It was a small thing, but interrogation was the art of building on weaknesses exposed through small things. For the same reason, his chair was a couple of inches higher than hers – nothing particularly noticeable but, again, designed to give him that slight psychological edge. That was part of the reason for using this chamber, too. Although nobody had been tortured there in his lifetime (Fouché wasn't even sure that anybody ever had been) the room's reputation gave it an atmosphere that somehow unnerved prisoners. In any case, the *Tour Bonbec* appealed to the traditionalist in Fouché.

Had William been there to see her, he would have realised that something – the chamber, the height of the chair or, more probably, the sense that she faced execution – was terrifying Pascale. When Fouché left a pause in his interrogation, she could sit silently for a minute or more before speaking and her laughter was almost entirely absent. To Fouché – who had never seen her chatting merrily about nothing for hours on end, always cheerful and laughing – to him, she seemed remarkably calm. Perhaps it was the notion that she would be more amenable to questioning after another night in her cell, rather than any lingering chivalric impulse that made him cut the questioning short.

The one calling himself Julien was next. A solid looking man, Fouché thought, maybe ex-military. He tried asking him about his background in France. "I am loyal to King Louis," the man said.

Fouché sighed. Obviously he was loyal to the Bourbon king. Why else did he think he was a prisoner in the Conciergerie? His little gesture of defiance achieved nothing except to offer a starting point for Fouché's questioning.

How had he expressed that loyalty? Had he served in the army? The navy? No answer, but Fouché felt in his water that the man had military experience. He had learned to trust his instincts in such matters.

"You are familiar with machines of war, I think."

A flicker of emotion. Yes! This man was one of the wretches that made those infernal machines that wreaked such havoc on the innocent citizenry of France.

"We will wait, *mon ami,* and when men follow you, carrying the explosive and the fuses and we have your infernal machine, then you will find I am not so gentle. These men –" he gestured to the guards – "will be delighted to mete out justice to those who devise such horrors. But you can atone for your sin." His years with the Oratorians had left him with clear views on sin and atonement. "If you confess everything now, you can yet save yourself – not only spiritually but in your body. You can yet escape a beating."

Fouché could see it in his eyes: the flicker of fear; the first beginnings of doubt. Now was not the time to push. Now he would step away and allow that first flicker to grow into a flame that would consume his courage. There was no hurry. These three weren't going anywhere. They had searched the heels of their shoes – even the woman's shoes – and found the blades hidden there. Nobody was going to escape the way that wretched painter had.

He clicked his fingers and the guards lifted Julien from his seat and started back towards the cells.

One more interview and he would make his way to bed. He yawned. What was the next fellow's name? Fabrice, that was it.

A few questions, a threat or two, and he would be done for the night. He yawned again. No matter: there was no hurry.

63

CHAPTER 14: The morning after

Burke woke late the next morning in a tangle of bedsheets. Amelie's head was resting on his chest and her fingers were tracing patterns along his arms.

He turned towards her and their lips touched – and then a clock on a table across the room began to chime.

"*Sacrebleu!* Is that the time already? I have to get up. I'm supposed to be attending on the Empress at noon and she is so bad tempered these days."

"I thought everything was going well with the Empire."

"With the Empire, yes. With the Emperor, no. They are on the verge of divorce. That awful man Fouché has been making trouble."

"What on earth has it to do with the Minister of Police?"

Amelie was already out of bed, rummaging through a chest of clothes. Satin and silk flew in all directions.

"Oh, you know Fouché." She paused for a moment and looked up at him. "I suppose you don't, being Irish." She bent back to the clothes but kept talking and she searched. "He likes to think of himself as guiding the Empire. The power behind the throne and such. He's decided that it would be a good thing for France – and hence M Fouché – if the Emperor married into one of the great royal families of Europe, and that means persuading Napoleon to abandon poor Josephine."

She emerged from the chest holding a yellow dress somewhat more substantial than the one she had been wearing the previous night and which was now lying crumpled by the bed. "Damn! The trouble with living in an apartment like this is that I can't afford my own maid. Can you help me, *chérie*?"

James had undressed enough women to know his way round fashionable clothes. Amelie's outfit was hardly, in any case, a challenge. She had a chemise (noticeably absent the night before) and some fine silk stockings, but otherwise he had only to cope with her dress. A column of tiny hook-and-eye fastenings closed it up her spine. Burke struggled to fix each one. They were designed for a maid's delicate hands rather than his thick fingers and somehow much more difficult to fasten in the morning than they were to remove the night before.

"How do you manage when there isn't a man here to help you?"

She gave him a particularly charming smile. "There usually seems to be someone about."

Even Burke was, for a moment, shocked and she relented. "There are a few other women in these apartments. Some even have a maid. I can drift around respectably enough in my robe until I find someone in who will help. And, if not, I have a couple of dresses that fasten with ties at the front." She smiled again. "Honestly, James, I did not bring you here simply to assist me with my dressing."

She smoothed down the dress and looked critically at herself in a mirror in an ornate wooden frame. "Not too bad." She gestured to James. "Can you pass me another pair of gloves? They're in that drawer." Last night's gloves lay with the other discarded clothes on the floor. James wondered if they would be worn again. Women, it seemed to him, could run through an astonishing number of gloves in just a few weeks.

When he turned back to Amelie she was adjusting her bonnet – a curious affair designed to look like a turban rather than a conventional hat. It was, Burke thought, an unusual sort of head-gear but rather charming. A few of her chestnut curls slipped out below the brim. On an impulse he leaned forward and kissed her.

"*Oh là.* Do be careful of the bonnet. It sits well, no?"

James assured her that it did and she rewarded him with a careful kiss on his forehead.

"Will I see you tonight?"

Burke assured her gravely that she would, if he only knew where she might be found.

"Oh goodness." There were some invitation cards propped on the mantelpiece. She took one and, at a bureau tucked away in a corner, she snatched at what Burke took to be a pen and scribbled something on the invitation.

Burke shook his head. She seemed a bright girl, but he was hardly going to be able to read what she had written if she didn't get her pen in the ink.

She turned and passed the card to him. His name had been firmly written at the top with a note to say that Amelie would be most obliged if he could attend. The writing was clear and black. It looked like pencil but there was something not quite right about it and the neatly sharpened stick she tossed back on the bureau looked like no pencil he had ever seen.

Seeing at the confusion on his face, she laughed. "It's one of Conté's new pencils. He invented them once the English cut off our graphite supplies. Napoleon thinks they are wonderful and insists on them being distributed all round the Tuileries. They are useful in my boudoir, aren't they? A girl can't risk getting ink on a new dress."

She blew him another kiss and headed for the door. "Let yourself out. I'll trust you not to steal anything. And make sure you are at the party tonight."

And, in a rustle of silk, she was gone.

* * *

James dressed slowly before leaving Amelie's apartment and heading back to his hotel. He was relieved to notice that he was not the only gentleman wearing evening clothes and dancing pumps, but he was still happy to get back to his room and to change into something that didn't advertise that he had not slept in his own bed the previous night.

William was waiting for him, looking nauseatingly wide-awake and cheerful for a man who Burke was confident had been drinking until almost dawn.

"I trust you had a useful night."

"Fairly useful. There's a few here invalided back from Spain. We exchanged our memories of Talavera. 'Course my memories had to be adapted a bit."

"Of course."

"We all agreed it was a famous victory. I'd like to say that I had my fingers crossed and was thinking of our lads, but listening to the French, I think they might be right. You know they marched in pretty well as soon as we pulled out?"

"Yes, William. It was the subject of frequent discussion in Merida."

"Damn shame."

William had told him about young Peters who had lost his leg at Talavera and all the others whose names he had never even had time to learn. The French had climbed the hill up to the British lines again and again. They had never seemed to know it was impossible to take that position and, in their ignorance, they had come close to taking it. So many dead on both sides! And nothing achieved by it.

Officer and man sat in silence for a moment and then, shaking himself as if to shake off his memories of that day, Brown carried on with his news of the night before.

"The Conciergerie is mainly offices, so most of the people in there are civilians, but there are some soldiers. There are all sorts and some of those who were wounded in Spain have been found jobs there. They guard the entrances and keep an eye on the safety of the people inside. There are a few important men, who they reckon need protecting. Mainly Fouché, of course. The Minister of Police is not a popular man."

"I believe so. Even the smart set at the party were complaining about him."

"Well he's not guarded by wounded warriors. There are gendarmes who do his dirty work and they watch out for unwanted visitors as well. Then there's guards for the prisoners. They aren't from the gendarmerie, who think themselves above that sort of work, but they aren't half-crippled either. Regular infantry."

"Now it gets more interesting. Where are the cells? I was told last night that the prisoners used to sleep in the corridors, but things have apparently changed since those days."

"Yes. There was one old guy who claimed to remember back then. He says that they packed all the women into one corridor and all the men into another. They weren't usually there for long. The Revolutionary Tribunals didn't hang about."

Burke nodded. That fitted well enough with what he had been told the night before.

"Now they have a row of cells near the court where they hold prisoners who are being tried there. They don't stay there any time really – they usually come in from other prisons and are transferred out again after their cases are heard. But tucked away in a corner there are some other cells for what my new mates called "politicals" which presumably includes suspected spies. They had cells for special cases back in the Terror and they use those. Seems my travelling companions may be banged up where Marie Antoinette spent her last days next to the infirmary, just in case. They didn't want her getting sick before they murdered her."

"How very considerate." Burke pondered William's information. "That's definitely progress of a sort. Did you hear anything about Empress Josephine and a divorce?"

"I heard a good few dirty songs featuring the woman. People say that things between her and old Boney aren't going too well but it's all just gossip and dirty jokes. Did the swells at your party know anything more?"

Burke told him what he had learned about Fouché's interference in Napoleon's marriage. "It was probably the most interesting thing I learned last night. Otherwise I met a few fellows who might be able to help. Most of them seem to sell stuff to the government fairly regularly and aren't too concerned about where it came from. If they are supplying the government they might have contacts I can use. It will all take time, though. I think my best bet may well be the girl."

"How do you think she will be able to help?"

"She's one of the Empress's young women. If Josephine and Napoleon are getting divorced, there is going to be a lot of money involved – an awful lot. And because Napoleon is, to all intents and purposes, the State, a lot of it will be government money. Which suggests to me that there is likely to be a fair bit of going and coming between Josephine's people and the government offices – including, I hope, offices in the Conciergerie. If I can persuade any of my new friends at court that I should be part of those comings and goings, I might be one step nearer getting myself into the place. It seems our best chance."

William looked sceptical. "How do you think you're going to do that?"

"I can't say I have a plan as such." He was unusually diffident. "More, perhaps, the sketch of an idea of a plan."

William allowed his doubts to show in the way he scratched his chin. "And where do you think we can start with this idea of a sketch of a whatever?"

"Oh, that's easy." Burke's natural confidence was reasserting itself. "Young Amelie runs with a smart set and I must dress to impress. We must start with another visit to my tailor!"

* * *

The life of a spy, Burke thought to himself, is not all about cunning plans and dangerous escapades. Much of it is about mundane matters like having the right clothes for a party. William had told him about Pascale and the selection of dresses she had had carried up the cliff-face in Normandy. He was coming round to the idea that her priorities had been entirely correct. Not that her wardrobe was going to help her in the Conciergerie.

The tailor had looked momentarily alarmed to see them again, obviously worried that a return visit so soon must have been occasioned by some complaint about his previous day's efforts. Once reassured, though, he was happy to promise another outfit. Burke indicated a roll of fabric. Could it be in that particular shade of blue? It was not just that he liked the colour – it meant that the tailor would not be able to make changes to something already started. The man had done good work the day before, but Burke expected even better this time.

The tailor hesitated, but barely for a moment. The ready money, Burke knew, was the decisive factor. Most of his customers would be local and hence, ostensibly, good for credit. Tailors' bills, though, were easily overlooked. A gentleman who paid cash was always worthy of extra consideration.

His wardrobe attended to, Burke decided to concentrate on the inner man. The Parisian aristocracy was as unwilling to rise early as the aristocracy in London and their indolence seemed to be trickling down throughout the population. Although the morning was half over, it was still a perfectly acceptable time to have breakfast, so Burke set off to explore the cafés in the area while William vanished away to find a suitable bar for a working man with a half day to kill.

Burke took his time over a drink of hot chocolate and a brioche before making a round of visits to some of his new friends from the previous night. They seemed happy enough to see him and there was talk of possible ventures involving all sorts of things that the French would like to see travelling by night across the Channel. Pencil leads, it seemed, were one of a growing list of items that Napoleon was finding it increasingly difficult to get hold of. Burke was pleased to learn at first-hand how effective England's economic blockade was proving, but the talk showed no sign of any ideas sufficiently advanced to get him into government offices at the speed he needed if he was to be able to save the prisoners in the Conciergerie. He would waste no more effort on the merchants. Instead, he decided, he would call on his tailor.

The visit to the tailor was an unalloyed pleasure after a frustrating afternoon. The man greeted him as a long-lost friend. Would he like coffee? Should he send out for some cake? Burke declined the cake but enjoyed the coffee, sipping from a tiny cup while the tailor produced a coat that Burke admitted to himself was almost the equal of anything he would be able to buy in London. The man hummed cheerfully as he marked some slight alterations with his chalk and pinned a little at the waist. Burke admired his appearance in the mirror. The man had done an excellent job. Amelie, he hoped, would be impressed.

It was once again agreed that William would collect the clothes that evening at ten, leaving Burke to rest and take some light refreshment ahead of the night's entertainment.

Some time later, after a light supper of omelette and oysters and a couple of hours sleep, James woke to find William hanging his new clothes ready for him to put on.

CHAPTER 15: Another party (but this time with an invitation)

Tonight, Burke had an address and an invitation. He also had a new and subtly more expensive outfit, delivered by William on the dot of ten. William had also arranged the hire of a carriage. It was important to look like a man of means and not an adventurer and James thought that Colonel Gordon would consider carriage hire a sensible use of his money.

This party was further from the centre – out in the Faubourg St Michel near the Luxembourg Palace. As his carriage clattered over the old Pont Neuf, Burke caught a glimpse of the lights of the Conciergerie over on his left and wondered if he would ever be able to bluff his way in.

Tonight he could afford to arrive at a more fashionable hour and the room was crowded as he entered. Josephine and her party, though, had not yet arrived. He exchanged greetings with some of the men he had met the night before and fought off the attentions of two or three determined young ladies. Clearly the revolution had consigned the idea of maidenly modesty firmly to the category of counter-revolutionary behaviour. Burke, though, could not afford to succumb to their charms. He was saving himself for Amelie.

It was not until midnight that the Empress and her entourage arrived at the party. While there was no formal ceremony – no trumpeters, no announcement of her arrival – the room fell briefly silent. Men bowed and women curtsied. Burke, whose own bow was exceptionally deep, marvelled at the degree to which the court of Napoleon had taken on the trappings of the monarchy that had been so bloodily overthrown.

He was pleased to see Amelie looking around, trying to spot him. When she did, her face lit up with a smile and she beckoned him to join her.

He made his way through the crowd which had, after that momentary pause, returned to their conversations and dancing.

As he reached the group around the Empress one gorgeously attired army officer took a pace towards him. "Excuse me, sir, but if you could return –"

Before he could finish his sentence Amelie was at his side explaining that Burke was her guest. The officer bowed his apologies and moved away and Burke found himself following Amelie towards the Empress. To his astonishment, Josephine greeted him by name.

"Ah, M de Burgh. I am so happy to see you here. You have quite turned our Amelie's head."

The Empress was well into her forties now, but the beauty that had made her the toast of Paris twenty years earlier still lingered. She was quite tall – probably an inch or two taller than Napoleon, which must, Burke thought, annoy the Corsican tyrant. Her hair was still dark and curled to her head. She was slim, but with magnificent breasts. Burke was relieved to see that, unlike so many of the younger ladies, she was respectably covered but he could well believe that in her younger days her charms were, as so often rumoured in London, enjoyed by many of the men of Paris.

"Amelie says you are a man of business." Her voice was slightly husky and the way she said 'man of business' suggested that it was a term that could encompass all sorts of things. That was, of course, why Burke described himself that way but, as Josephine said it, it summoned up possibilities that Burke did not usually associate with the phrase.

He agreed that he was, indeed, a 'man of business' and he felt himself blush as he said so.

"You are an Irishman, she tells me. You must be good at negotiating through all manner of difficult waters."

It was odd, Burke thought, that while smuggling was such a significant business and smuggled produce was so widely traded, nobody ever liked to use the word. 'Difficult waters' indeed. But it did allow him to suggest that his negotiating skills went far beyond the arrangements for the shipment of Irish whiskey or French brandy. His services, he indicated, were used to assist his friends in all sorts of situations: contract disputes, property arguments, even divorces.

He was conscious of a nervous silence from many of the ladies around the Empress and he wondered if he had gone too far but Josephine responded with a tired smile.

"If only I had a friend who could arrange such details. I am, as you may have heard, hard pressed in some delicate negotiations of my own. I wonder what you can bring to them that my own agents cannot – for I must admit I am not sure that they apply themselves to the issues as enthusiastically as I might wish."

"Your Imperial Majesty," he bowed slightly, "my efforts are untainted by loyalty to anyone but my client. And," he favoured her with a roguish smile, "I cheat."

The Empress did not smile back. "This is not the place for such depressing matters," she said, and turned away. For a moment Burke thought that he had pushed his luck too far, but then, as Josephine passed Amelie she said, quietly, "Bring M de Burgh to our chambers tomorrow," and then she was talking to one of the other ladies about a shawl she had just had delivered to Paris from Persia. Her triumph over her husband's restrictions on imported silk clearly delighted her and Burke heard her laugh. It was a clear laugh – that of a much younger woman and someone who one would think had not a care in the world.

Amelie, who had stood carefully away from James as he talked with Josephine now reclaimed him, coiling her arm around his.

"Your Empress," he remarked, "is a cleverer woman than she likes men to imagine."

Amelie smiled disingenuously. "So are most women, my dear." And then, "Shouldn't you be asking me to dance?"

CHAPTER 16: *La Tour Bonbec* – second night

"I think you are not a bad person," he said.

Pascale smiled at him. It was hard work, that smile. But she made it look natural. She was *une jolie jeune fille*, not a prisoner facing the most feared man in France.

"I think you are not a bad person either." That was a lie. She thought he was the most bad person she had ever met, ever imagined meeting.

"I think you are just a pretty face. You are here to draw attention from those who do the real work: the truly dangerous ones."

Stupid man! She kept the smile on her face, but inside she was seething. "No!" she wanted to shout. "They draw attention away from me. I am the truly dangerous one. They will kill ten people, twenty people, a hundred people. What difference will it make? It will only strengthen the belief of the French people that their enemies are monsters who must be resisted to the last man." Whereas she – her cartoons mocked Napoleon; her pamphlets told mothers that their sons were dying in pointless wars. The scurrilous verses so carefully composed by men in London who knew how to poison the minds of the people – they were the way the war would be won.

Inside, she was angry, but she still smiled. She even managed a little laugh – though William would never have recognised it alongside the unforced good humour of their journey to Paris.

"Dangerous! Julien and Fabrice? I can't believe it!"

"They are, ma'amselle, believe me."

He watched her: saw the disbelief in her eyes. Could he be mistaken? Could she be the innocent she appeared to be? Surely not.

He should have her beaten. They should use the clubs and the cudgels. They should insult her sex.

He closed his eyes a moment. No: that would not do. He would start with the men.

"Take her back to her cell. Bring the prisoner Julien in."

That was best. She could wait. He was in no hurry.

CHAPTER 17: An interview with an Empress

The ridiculous gilt clock on Amelie's mantel woke Burke as it chimed twelve. "Good heavens, is that the time?"

Amelie wriggled against him. "No, silly. It was about an hour fast yesterday, so it's probably even further off today. If it kept proper time do you think it would have been given to me for this room?"

She stretched, arching her back and throwing her arms out from the tangle of sheets. "Still it must be almost eleven. You'd best be going."

"Really?" Burke thought she was just teasing and reached an arm around her, but she pushed him away.

"Yes, really. The Empress receives at four in the afternoon. You must be there and, beautiful as you are, you need to be dressed in suitable clothing for court. You need to see your valet and, maybe, your tailor."

James sighed. Amelie's judgement was harsh, but fair. He could hardly turn up at the Tuileries wearing clothes from the night before.

He dressed quickly and hurried to his hotel. A boy summoned William from the garret room he shared with half a dozen other servants and soon James and his sergeant were urgently reviewing his wardrobe.

"With the best will in the world, I don't think you can get a new suit of clothes made up by this afternoon," said William.

Burke nodded in reluctant agreement. "A new shirt, though, I think. And a fresh stock. You can take this one and starch it, but we need something new for this afternoon."

"And a new cravat, I think."

Burke nodded. Brown's role as his valet might often be a cover for his espionage activities, but he took the business seriously and Burke was always happy to take his advice on such matters.

"Gloves too," Burke added to the list. "Fresh gloves, a new shirt and cravat, we can get away with the jacket I wore on the first day. New stockings, of course, and breeches if they can manage those within two hours. Trousers seem more the fashion, but the court may well be more formal and they aren't going to make me a new pair of trousers by this afternoon. I had best order a new coat and shoes for tomorrow. I don't want to be caught out like this again."

The two men went together to the tailor: no gentleman would leave the choice of a coat fabric and lining to his valet, but William was to fetch and carry and could be trusted on details like the choice of stock. "High and white, William, that's all I ask."

By now the tailor was happy to extend a line of credit, which was useful as Gordon's supply of gold was dwindling. Burke made a mental note that an evening of high stakes whist might be in order.

Burke left William choosing a stock and gathering up packages while he went back to his hotel. He hesitated as to whether or not he should bath again – it was, after all, only a couple of days since the last time he had indulged and he shared the common concern that too much bathing could damage your internal organs. On the other hand, he was to attend on the Empress. He realised that French notions of personal hygiene could leave something to be desired (he blamed their obsession with garlic) but felt that, as an Englishman, he should be seen to uphold a higher standard than the average Parisian. A bath was therefore ordered and the procession of servants arrived again. Burke suspected that there may have been one or two more this time, drawn by the novelty of a guest bathing twice in the same week, but they were once again all shooed out. He even managed – eventually – to persuade the maid that his tip on the previous occasion was not intended as an inducement for her to share his bath with him.

By the time William returned, Burke was clean, refreshed and ready to dress himself for a meeting with the Empress. He allowed William to fuss over him with a clothes brush, pulling at a seam here and tugging a hem there until Brown announced that he considered Burke ready for elegant society. At least, James thought, he did not have to fuss about with a wig: the revolution seemed to have got rid of at least that antediluvian hazard to a man dressing in a hurry.

He strolled easily from his rooms to the Tuileries where, on giving his name to the guard at the door, he was moved smoothly from flunky to flunky, up splendid staircases and along endless corridors. The liveried servants reminded him of his visit to the Spanish court, but the servants here seemed more controlled. The whole place had the air of an establishment run on discipline and order.

Josephine's apartments, when he arrived there, seemed at first to offer a more relaxed, feminine ambience. She sat surrounded by a semi-circle of ladies, including Amelie, who gave James an encouraging smile but remained sitting at her place. There were a few men who seemed to be there on business with the Empress. As Burke entered one of them was asking Josephine to intervene to allow a cargo of silks to be offloaded in Marseilles. She was clearly sympathetic but pointed out that her husband had forbidden such imports. Then she (rather unsubtly, Burke thought) adjusted the silk shawl she was wearing. The merchant looked puzzled for a moment and then, suddenly realising what was required, explained that if his cargo would be landed he would, of course, be delighted to make a gift of a bolt or two of silk to the ladies of the court. Josephine smiled pleasantly and said she would see what she could do.

Another couple of gentlemen muttered their requests quietly so that Burke was unable to hear, but both seemed happy enough with her response. Each bowed and left and Burke realised that he was now the only man left in the room.

Josephine clapped her hands and made a gentle shooing motion. "Off you go, ladies. I need to speak to M de Burgh in confidence." The women rose is a susurration of dresses. It made Burke think of a flock of butterflies suddenly rising from a bush. "Not you, Amelie. You can remain to chaperone our guest. I wouldn't want it said that I had taken advantage of him."

There was polite laughter as the ladies left but James noticed that Amelie looked quite relieved. Burke wondered if a chaperone was a useful precaution. Josephine, though, was the perfect hostess. Amelie poured hot chocolate for James and presented him with petit fours to nibble while Josephine chatted about the previous night's party, the weather and Burke's first impressions of Paris.

"You are new to Paris, are you not, M de Burgh?"

Yes, Burke said. He had never visited before.

"And yet you suggest that you can assist people with the most delicate of business here."

The elegant lady of fashion was suddenly replaced by a shrewd woman who had been an Empress for five years and at the heart of European power for even longer. Amelie, without being asked, moved to a seat nearer the door, leaving Burke and Josephine to talk more privately.

Josephine had been, she said, impressed with his little speech the night before. She was, as she was sure he knew, engaged in delicate negotiations with Napoleon who was anxious to get divorced so that he could marry a younger woman who might bear him an heir.

"It is all he talks about," she said. Burke thought he saw a sheen of tears in her eyes. "How he must have a son to rule France when he dies."

In theory Josephine was well placed to negotiate a good divorce settlement. Napoleon wanted the divorce to be quick and simple and, as far as possible, amicable. He was also, by nature, given to spectacularly generous gestures. But his years as ruler of France had also taught him to be a cautious administrator, who could be obsessive about small economies.

"So he says that if he were to abandon me, I would be given the Chateau of Malmaison to live in. But then he says that the employment of the servants would be my responsibility to bear from my own allowance." She blinked away her tears. "Monsieur, Malmaison is not a small home. There is the garden. There are the animals. These need to be paid for. To give me the house alone is to chain a rock around my neck."

Burke nodded sympathetically. But surely, he suggested, that rather depended on how high the allowance was.

And there was the nub of Josephine's problem. She had no idea how much Napoleon could afford.

It seemed ridiculous but, as Josephine explained her predicament, it clearly was not. Napoleon might be the ruler of France, but he did not have infinite funds. He had been at war for all but one of the years of his rule and wars were expensive. He felt the need to impress other monarchs – monarchs whose right to their thrones was unquestioned. So his court had to be more splendid than those of the kings and princes he dealt with as they came to Paris to sign peace treaties or form new alliances. The army of flunkies Burke had remarked as he moved through the Tuileries was not just an extravagant luxury but an important symbol of Napoleon's position in the world. And this all cost money – money that was sometimes in short supply.

"I need to know," Josephine demanded, "how much money Napoleon has available for the divorce. And then I want every last franc of it."

So, Burke suggested, what she needed was sight of Napoleon's household accounts. They were presumably kept in some of the hundreds of offices in the Tuileries.

Josephine shook her head. "I can enter all of the offices here. And I have." She grinned – a surprisingly impish grin in an Empress. "Napoleon once told me I could not enter one of the offices and I threw a vase at him. It missed – really I was not trying to hit him – but it shattered into a thousand pieces. It was a Chinese vase and apparently cost rather more than I would have thought sensible. The Emperor was not pleased. After that, though, he did not try to stop me looking about the offices."

"I am sure you were most thorough."

"Indeed." Josephine raised her eyebrows and made a tiny moue of her lips – careful not to reveal her rotten teeth. "I saw not even a notebook, let alone the accounts themselves which must take up whole rooms. There will be a small army of clerks keeping track of the expenditure. The books are not kept in the Tuileries."

"In the Conciergerie, then?"

She nodded. "Of course. And I can hardly search there. It would not be seemly."

"But I could."

"If you had a reason to be allowed in."

It was, indeed, a poser. Burke looked around him, searching for inspiration. The room reflected the opulence that Burke had already come to associate with the Emperor. Fine paintings hung from the picture rails, beautiful *objets d'art* were placed here and there on ornamental side tables. He was not surprised that Napoleon was anxious to discourage his wife from throwing things at the walls. The contents of this one room alone must be worth a fortune.

And now an idea was forming.

"Tell me, your Majesty, when was there last an inventory at Malmaison?"

The Empress frowned, though she was careful (from force of habit, Burke presumed) to frown prettily.

"I'm not sure. A few years ago, I suppose. Why? Does it matter?"

"Where would the inventory records have been stored?"

Grand houses like Malmaison, he knew, were inventoried regularly with a record of every chair, every table, every painting, every snuffbox. The records, kept room by room, could fill many volumes and would be stored safely – ideally away from the house in question. There was no point in having an inventory that could be lost alongside the property being inventoried.

The Empress's frown vanished and she began to smile. "I believe they are kept in the Conciergerie."

The rest of the plan was simple. Josephine would conduct a fresh inventory of Malmaison – a natural thing to do in the light of the divorce negotiations. She would order it started immediately and, as each room was inventoried, Burke would be despatched to the Conciergerie to compare the results of the latest inventory with that of the previous one and report on any discrepancies. It would be a long job and he would be in and out of the Conciergerie every day.

CHAPTER 18: Office of the Minister of Police, Paris

Fouché sat at his desk writing another of his interminable reports to the Emperor. There were those who thought report writing was the boring bit of intelligence work. That's why they continued to be minor provincial officials while he ran the Empire. Well, the French bit of it anyway. Napoleon did the army and the endless wars, but he ran France. Only it was, perhaps, wisest to let Napoleon think the Emperor did.

He had to admit that Napoleon's eye for detail was remarkable and his demand for trivia almost insatiable. There was a woman in Lyons who had remarked that getting workers on the farm was almost impossible with so many young men away in the army and that Louis might have been a fat bastard but that at least he left the villagers alone to bring in the harvest. Napoleon might well be interested in that. Fouché wondered how he would respond – if he responded at all. It all depended on his mood. He might send a few soldiers to Lyons to help out with agricultural matters or he might order a new tax inspection in which it was likely that the stupid woman would lose whatever savings she had squirrelled away and quite possibly her farm as well.

Fouché shrugged. He didn't care about the woman in Lyon. Napoleon could entertain himself with her. He had bigger fish to fry -- like the spies that had been brought to the Conciergerie two days ago.

So far he had learned nothing. Clearly, they had been trained, presumably by the English. They had given their names, which matched those on the documents they carried, but Fouché was confident that these were not their real names. Where did they come from? From the Vendome, they said – and their papers backed them up. Fouché was certain they had started their journey in England. The girl had some pamphlets when she was captured and surely there must be more somewhere – hidden away for her to collect or following on with some messenger. The pamphlets, he was sure, had come from England. They could not have been printed in France, for any printer responsible for such treasonous rubbish would have been identified and arrested long ago.

Beyond their false names and their fictitious addresses, he had nothing. Why were they in Paris? Just travelling – they had always wanted to see the capital. Where had they visited on their journey? Don't really remember – nowhere that stuck in the mind. Nothing could be achieved by subtlety faced with this sort of obstinacy.

Somewhere he heard a clock striking three. He finished writing and called for one of the secretaries who would stay through the night, ready to respond whenever he ordered them into action.

"Have this taken to the Emperor. And send down to the cells. Wake the two men I interviewed yesterday and start beating them. I'll call for them tomorrow and I want them softened up by then."

CHAPTER 19: A respectable interlude

Burke woke late and alone. He was at his hotel, having spent much of the night at cards.

William has recommended a card school that he had discovered while Burke had been out partying. Burke had been sceptical. He needed to top up Gordon's cash and that meant playing for serious money. His experience was that serious money meant aristocrats or military officers. With the best will in the world he didn't see William being able to introduce him into the kind of game he was looking for.

"You're forgetting there's been a revolution," William reminded him. "It's like with any revolution." William had seen a couple of uprisings from ground level in the past few years and he reckoned he knew what he was talking about. "Most of the poor stay poor. A lot get poorer. But a few can suddenly find themselves coming into money. And those are the ones playing Quadrille at the Inn of the Tin Plate."

"Unusual name."

"It's an old name. It's an old inn."

"Hmm." Burke did not look happy.

"You do know how to play Quadrille, don't you, sir?"

Burke grimaced. "It's a horrible game and everywhere you go people have their own rules, but I can play it at a push. And it only uses 40 cards, so that makes it that much easier to cheat."

"I wouldn't know, sir. I leave the card-sharping to you."

Now, stretching in bed and wishing his head would stop aching, Burke decided that Quadrille was an excellent game. William had kept buying everybody drinks and Burke had kept carefully spilling his on the floor while attention was on the game and what with his natural skill at cards, his ruthless cheating and the fact that everybody else there was helplessly drunk by midnight, he did not anticipate any financial problems for a while. He would have to avoid the 'Tin Plate' in future, though. If the gamblers there remembered anything of the evening once they were sober, they might wonder just how they had lost so comprehensively. Still, the *arrondissement* where Jacques Berthout had spent the night winning a small fortune was far from the areas that M de Burgh might expect to be seen in, so Burke had few worries about being recognised.

There was a very gentle knock at the door and it opened to reveal William bearing a small tray with a cup of coffee. He looked, Burke thought, quite ridiculously up to snuff after the night before – but then William's ability to be unaffected by alcohol never ceased to amaze him.

"I thought you might appreciate the coffee, sir. I'd bring tea, but this not being a civilised country …" He let his remark tail off. There was, after all, little that could be said about the inadequacies of the French that he had not said already.

Burke took the coffee gratefully. He allowed a few minutes for it to begin to take effect and then started gingerly to get out of bed. William helped him dress and then, walking slowly and trying not to move his head at all, Burke made his way to a restaurant.

The place was busy and Burke could have done without the din created by a couple of hundred customers, but the food was good and the wine was cheap and half an hour later he was finishing his second coffee of the day and feeling considerably more like his usual self.

The first thing he would have to do, he decided, was to make his peace with Amelie. She had been less than pleased when he had announced that he needed to return to his hotel after his meeting with Josephine, although she was somewhat mollified by the idea that his nights with her had left him so exhausted that he needed a night alone to catch up on his sleep. Jewellery, he thought, would be an appropriate peace offering: something that would go well with yellow. A visit to a jeweller was called for. His winnings would not stretch to yellow emeralds, but he found some yellow topaz earrings that looked pretty enough and, thus armed, he made his way to the Tuileries.

The guards at the door checked his name against a list, which he thought was startlingly efficient. He was nodded through and again, passed from flunky to flunky until he arrived at Josephine's court. There he was relieved to see Amelie sitting demurely with the Empress's other ladies and even prepared to offer him a small smile.

He carried the package from the jeweller neatly tied up with a satin bow. Josephine, who he suspected could detect the presence of jewellery at a hundred paces, remarked on it almost immediately. Had M de Burgh brought a gift for her little Amelie? He must present it to her at once.

There was much fluttering amongst the other ladies and Amelie blushed most becomingly. The gift was duly presented and unwrapped. There was perhaps the faintest disappointment among some of the other ladies when the stones were revealed as topaz. Burke did wonder if he shouldn't just have committed himself to another night of gambling and tried for the emeralds, but Amelie looked happy and Josephine honoured the couple with an approving smile. To his relief, his choice of gift seemed to have been approved by the two women in the room whose opinion mattered to him.

Once the ladies had been sent on their way and Josephine was able to turn to business, it was clear that she was happy with the way his plans were going. The housekeeper at Malmaison had started on the smallest rooms and Burke already had an inventory of the billiard room which, being dominated by a billiard table, had relatively little other furniture.

"I have attached an authority for you to enter the Conciergerie for you to compare it with the previous itinerary. When do you think you will start?"

Burke suggested he go there that afternoon. This was the fourth night the prisoners would have been held. If Burke was doing the interrogating he would work at night when the prisoners' resistance was lowest. How many nights could they hold out? If they had not talked yet, they were bound to break soon. Burke knew he had little time. And starting work late in the afternoon meant that he might be able to work late in the building when there would be fewer people around and he would be able to move about more easily – both searching for details of Napoleon's household expenditure and for a way for the prisoners to escape.

"This afternoon it is, then." He was, he realised, being dismissed.

"And, M de Burgh, I will be sure to explain to little Amelie that it is my fault you will not see her tonight."

Burke bowed and left.

CHAPTER 20: The Conciergerie

Burke's letter of authority admitted him to the Conciergerie without any problems. The place was, after all, mainly office buildings.

He was directed along one corridor and then another; up one set of stairs and down a second before being told that he should climb a third and then ask for more directions. Like any building that has grown over hundreds of years and constantly evolved from fortress to royal residence to prison to offices, it was a jumble of bits added on and bits reshaped until it was a wonder that anyone could find anything at all.

Burke was delighted. He had every excuse for getting lost, giving him plenty of opportunity to explore the place. First, though, he did need to find the room with the inventories.

It took a while. Not because of any confusion on his part – his sense of direction was excellent – but because the office was so obscure that most of the clerks who directed him honestly had no idea of where it was. Eventually, though, he arrived at a small room – really little more than a cupboard – off a larger room which may once have been some sort of assembly hall but which was now filled with rows of desks where industrious scribes recorded – well, Burke had no idea what, but they recorded it most industriously. Burke wondered if it had anything to do with the vast French military machine that had been chewing up so much of Europe. He chuckled to himself at the thought, because one thing he knew about military records was that they seldom bore any relationship to the actual supplies available in the field. Still, it kept the scribes occupied, so, whatever they were recording, it served to keep their families fed.

The inventory books for Malmaison were thick with dust and were guarded by a clerk who seemed almost as dusty himself. He appeared happy to see Burke, though, and applied himself enthusiastically to working through the books to find the latest inventory for the billiard room. In fact he was so enthusiastic that it gradually dawned on Burke that the poor soul had probably been sitting there waiting for someone to show an interest in the records ever since the last inventory was conducted some years earlier.

Once the right volume had been found, Burke started to laboriously compare the old records with the ones he had just been given. Paper, ink and a quill pen appeared from a corner cupboard and Burke began to make notes. The billiard table was obvious enough, but what of the cues? There were no spares now. Had there been at the last inventory? Was there any record of cues broken or lost?

He worked on with equal thoroughness through the stools, the side tables, the ornamental vases, the paintings....

The evening was turning to night and the scribes next door were leaving for the day. Could he have a candle? Yes, there were candles here. The clerk searched again in his corner cupboard and found a candle, a candlestick and taper. "There should be a light burning in the corridor," he said. "I'll get a flame for you." He vanished away, returning several minutes later with the taper lit. From that he lit the candle, providing a little pool of light for Burke to read by.

Burke looked up from his notes as if he had only then noticed how dark it was getting. "Don't stay on my account," he said. "I'll make sure to leave the place tidy and the candle safely out."

The clerk looked around him as if checking to see if there was anything too precious to leave unguarded. Clearly there wasn't. "Well, if you're sure..."

Of course, Burke reassured him. It was fine. He'd be back the next day anyway.

The clerk left and Burke scribbled away at his notes until he could hear no movement in the rooms around. Then, leaving the candle safely out of any draughts and well clear of his paperwork, he set off to explore.

* * *

It's obvious that if you want information, the simplest way to get it is to ask somebody who knows. Amateur spies tend to forget this simple point. They search through waste baskets, they hide in alleys to watch people's movements, they intercept their post. Professional spies ask servants what they can tell about their masters. Sometimes they don't even have to offer them money. In fact, offering too much money is often counter-productive. People love to gossip but taking a substantial bribe makes the gossip look like betrayal and most people, in Burke's experience, are quite surprisingly loyal to spouses, masters and even kings.

As he wandered the corridors, Burke kept his eyes open for anyone else working late. It did not take long to find someone. In London the civil service was run by gentlemen and people went to bed at a civilised hour, but Napoleon was famous for holding meetings late at night and offices here had at least a few clerks at work at all times of day.

"Can you help me? I'm looking for the Emperor's household accounts."

A momentary suspicion, a glance at Burke's authority to see the inventories, and the young man he had accosted gave him the directions he needed. After all there was no reason why every clerk in the building should be aware that the inventory was stored separately from the accounts.

"You need to go to the end of the corridor and downstairs, then turn left and..."

Burke smiled pleasantly and set off.

It took almost ten minutes to get to the archives, but when he did he was astonished at the sight that met his eyes. He emerged from the shambling chaos of the main building into what had clearly been a church. Although it was not a high room, the proportions gave a sense of space. Candlelight reflected from gold paint on the arches supporting the ceiling. It was big enough for the corners to be lost in gloom and must have been quite beautiful before the Revolutionaries had driven out the priests and replaced them with paperwork. Now the nave was filled with bookcases and shelves had been fixed to the walls.

Burke walked confidently down the nave. This was not the moment to look as if he didn't belong. The clerks here would know exactly where the papers he needed would be stored but they would also be much more likely to question his right to be there. They certainly wouldn't be fooled by an authority to examine the inventories. The answer, as ever, was to look as if he so obviously belonged that nobody would think for an instant that he did not.

As he was passing one bookcase full of anonymous ledgers (he doubted anyone knew offhand what 'Gen Purp Dept 1445, 1806' meant), he stopped and took a volume off the shelf. Holding it under his arm, he walked on a few yards and took down another ledger.

Walking back towards the entrance he was no longer a stranger whose right of entry might be queried. He was a clerk who had been working in the depths of the building and had the ledgers to prove it.

Just inside the door was a railed off desk where an elderly man was busy annotating what looked to Burke like catalogue cards. This, he assumed, was the librarian.

"I'm sorry to bother you. I've just been referring to this ledger." He opened the first of the two volumes and pointed to one of the entries. "I was trying to cross reference this, but when I went to the 1446 shelf, I found this." He waved the second ledger. "It looks like accounts for the Emperor's household. Shouldn't this be stored in a separate section?"

"Indeed yes." The librarian dropped the catalogue cards onto his desk and looked at the book Burke was brandishing as if it were a personal affront. He stood and leaned across his desk as if to reach for it, but Burke held it beyond his grasp. He also took care not to show the spine with its reference number.

"If you tell me where it belongs I can re-shelve it for you."

For a moment he thought that the librarian would insist on re-shelving it himself, but at that moment the door opened and a man, gloriously attired in the uniform of a footman from the Tuileries rushed in. "We need the 1808 grain production figures. 1809 estimates if you have them. The Emperor…"

"Yes, yes, I'll fetch them." As the librarian set off at a half run along the corridor he gestured to Burke. "Up the stairs, by the statue of St Peter."

Burke turned in the direction that the librarian had gestured. In the corner there was a small arch and through it Burke could make out a spiral staircase, presumably to some sort of storage chamber up above.

He hurried up the steps and emerged into a space so vast that he paused a moment, hardly believing what he saw. This was clearly the church whose roof he had seen from the street when he first walked past the Conciergerie. It stretched up far beyond the light thrown by his candle. Even in that uncertain light, the place was beautiful.

Statues of the Apostles were arranged along the nave. Most showed signs of damage, presumably inflicted in the early years of the revolution. Several had lost their heads, but St Peter was still easily recognisable, gripping broken keys in one battered hand. He was surrounded by boxes. In the boxes were files, ledgers, more, smaller, boxes and loose sheets of paper.

Burke heard footsteps approaching and grabbed up one ledger dated 1808.

"Can I help you?"

The tone suggested that the man, who had hurried the length of the church to ask the question, was more concerned with what Burke was doing there than with any genuine desire to render assistance.

"No, I'm fine, thank you. I have what I need."

"But –"

Burke cut him off. "There's a messenger from the Tuileries downstairs. I don't have time to talk."

The closer to the truth a lie is, the more effective. In this case Burke's words were absolutely true and thus all the more convincing. The man hesitated and Burke was off.

He walked briskly, but did not run. He was a man in a hurry, not a thief or fugitive. Nobody called for him to stop or closed any doors against him, but he did not slow down until he was safely back with the Malmaison inventory. Only then did he stop to look at the ledger he had appropriated.

He turned the pages, trying to make sense of the figures. It looked as if it was a record of expenditure on fabric of some sort. Could it be curtains? Hardly: the quantities looked more like the amount of fabric you would need to equip an army to spend a winter under canvas. But he had been told these were household accounts. It didn't make sense.

He turned over a dozen more pages and now there were buttons and epaulettes – but the sheer quantity of gold thread showed it could hardly be a military purchase unless it was to equip the General Staff in their ceremonial uniforms. And it was then, at the thought of 'ceremonial uniforms' that Burke realised what he was reading. These were the records of the money spent on all those splendidly dressed flunkies who lined the corridors of the Tuileries. If Josephine wanted evidence of the scale of her husband's spending, these figures would come in very useful.

He stretched and rubbed his eyes. It had been a long day and the smoke from the candles (not the pure beeswax of the Tuileries) was beginning to irritate. He couldn't rest yet though. The search for Napoleon's accounts was a mere sideshow. The main business of the night had to be the prisoners and so far he had achieved nothing at all as far as they were concerned. Time, he knew, was running out. If they hadn't broken already, they would soon.

He set off again. This time asking a direct question about which way to go was probably inadvisable. "Excuse me, but can you tell me where the important prisoners are being kept?" was likely to raise suspicions that an authority to look for paperwork would hardly allay. William's efforts, though, meant that he knew the prisoners were being held near the infirmary. Perhaps that was the way forward.

He set out to wander the corridors again until he came across anyone else in the place. Though it was now close to midnight, it was not long before he came across a harassed looking clerk hurrying from one office to another.

"Can you help me?" Burke clutched pitifully at his stomach, wincing with pain. "I think I have eaten some bad mussels. I need an apothecary."

"These are court offices. You'll not find an apothecary here." He prepared to rush off again.

"Perhaps –" Burke sounded as pitiable as possible. "… in the infirmary."

"Maybe." He delayed just long enough to gesture back the way he had come. "End of the corridor, turn left, then right." And he was off, muttering something about idiots who don't take care of what they eat.

Burke shuffled along, giving his best imitation of a man at death's door, until the clerk was out of sight. Then he walked briskly to the end of the corridor, turned left and moved on rather more cautiously.

A few paces later and there was the turn to the left.

Burke should have been prepared for the sight of the infirmary after he had seen the way that the church had been converted to archives with bookcases and shelving simply set up in the middle of the old building. He supposed that there may have been some sort of provision for the sick in the old mediaeval Castle, but that had obviously been completely inadequate during the days of the Terror when the place was packed with prisoners so a proper modern infirmary had been set up. The problem of how to fit one into the old building was solved simply enough. Essentially they had built a giant cage inside one of the old halls of the castle. Burke emerged from the corridor to find that, while the wall on his right was still the original stone blocks of the castle, on his left there was a metal grille about three feet high with regular bars running up to the ceiling. Torches along the right-hand wall of the corridor provided the only light and through the bars he could just make out rows of beds.

As he carried on between the stone wall on one side and the bars on the other, he heard groans ahead of him. Peering beyond the light of the torch he saw that some of the beds were occupied and figures stirred and moaned restlessly in the dark.

Burke had only the vaguest notion of how the hospital system worked in Paris but he was aware that Napoleon's government presided over a bureaucratic system that operated hospitals around the city. It was unlikely that anyone who had the chance to be treated in one of the modern hospitals that the Revolutionaries had built would choose instead to attend this gloomy place. Prisoners, though, were clearly kept in a hospital readily to hand – hence the bars. When the likes of

TOM WILLIAMS

Marie Antoinette were housed here, having somewhere to treat the sick would have been politically essential. It would never have done for the Royal Family to die of gaol-fever before they could be taken out and executed on the guillotine. Now, though, the place must be practically deserted.

There was another groan in the darkness ahead of him. Might that be one of William's erstwhile companions? He wondered how close he was to the *Tour Bonbec*.

Moving forward, he could make out the far end of what he supposed he should think of as the ward. There was more light there – a dull glow from a lantern illuminating the face of an elderly man sitting at a desk. He seemed half asleep, but Burke assumed he had some medical skill – enough to prescribe something for food poisoning at least. He resumed his stumbling gait, clutching at his stomach as he moved beyond the light from the wall sconce.

At the end of the corridor, though, he was brought up short by a barred gate that blocked further progress. He rattled at it, hoping to attract the attention of the fellow in charge of the patients. Instead, a gendarme emerged from a doorway the other side of the gate. He was carrying a lantern and raised it to throw a decent light through the bars onto Burke. Burke let out a particularly pitiful moan and doubled over, concealing his face from the light as much as possible.

"What the hell do you think you're up to?" The gendarme appeared unaffected by Burke's misery.

"Bad mussels, your honour. If I don't get purged , I'm not sure I can make it home."

A voice called from the doorway the gendarme had come from: "What's going on?"

"Some poncey clerk with gut ache. Wants the apothecary."

"Does he look dangerous?"

The guard waved the lantern in the general vicinity of Burke's face.

"Harmless as they come."

"Let him through then. It's only one man."

There was a rattle of keys and the gate swung open.

This side of the infirmary had a stone wall – presumably the original wall of the hall. It must have been quite an imposing structure before the bars were added with a flagrant disregard for the medieval architecture. The wall that made up the other side of this new corridor was broken up with half a dozen solid looking wooden doors, each with a small grill at eye level. These, Burke supposed, were the cells.

On his left he passed a smaller doorway that had been crudely bricked up. Further on there was an oversized entrance which presumably had once been the way into a splendid hall.

The guard gestured towards the doorway and Burke limped his way there doubled over and groaning. Some of the groaning was genuine by now, anticipating what was to come.

88

The apothecary might have been old and had little interest in his patients, but he knew how to treat food poisoning. Burke had hoped he would get off with just an emetic. An emetic, though, was only the start of it. As he vomited into a bucket that from its smell had recently been used for other purposes, the apothecary asked where he lived.

Burke invented an address on the South Bank near to the Île de la Cité.

"Not too far then. Good."

He fumbled in a cupboard as Burke gave a final heave into the bucket.

"Take these."

He handed over two large blue pills and Burke obediently swallowed.

"Now hurry home. You'll need to be in your privy when those take effect. You've probably got ten minutes."

Burke left at speed.

CHAPTER 21: A cunning plan

When William arrived with his coffee the next morning, he was shocked at the state Burke was in.

"You look as if you need to see a doctor."

"I've seen a doctor. Now I just have to recover from the experience."

Burke drained the coffee and sent William away to find another cup. "And a large glass of water. And a raw egg."

By the time William returned, Burke was looking a bit better and after the second cup of coffee and the egg he was ready to tell his sergeant about his experience.

He skipped over the full horrors of the apothecary's 'cure' but gave William a detailed description of the arrangements for guarding the prisoners.

"The gate to the rest of the Conciergerie is guarded by at least two men. They don't stand guard at it, but there's no way you'd be able to open it without them noticing. They have a clear view along the corridor with the cells too. So we'd need to get past the gate, somehow put the guards out of action and then open the cells – and check that the people we're looking for aren't in the infirmary which, if they've been tortured, seems quite likely."

William pursed his lips. "Tricky," he said.

"Indeed. I had rather hoped you might have an idea."

"Well, we do know how to get past the first gate."

"We do?"

"The way you did last night. Say you need the infirmary."

Burke grimaced. "If that apothecary gets hold of me again, I'm not sure that I won't die in that place alongside the prisoners. In any case, I doubt he's going to believe that I managed to poison myself two days running."

"But suppose it isn't you that's sick?"

Burke's face creased into a smile.

"By George, William, I think you may have cracked it."

* * *

After an hour of running over the details of their plan and a long, slow lunch, Burke felt ready for anything. The plan, admittedly, was more a rough sketch than a finished oil painting and it relied to a worrying degree on them having luck on their side, but it was the best they were going to come up with in the time they had left.

BURKE AND THE PIMPERNEL AFFAIR

The prospect of a perilous night gave, Burke thought, a particular piquancy to an afternoon at Josephine's court. He made certain to arrive early. He wanted time to reassure Amelie that he was not neglecting her by choice.

He wanted to take her jewellery, but he did not dare risk the humiliation of his gift being compared with the stones worn by the other ladies of Josephine's court. He would have to rely on his charm.

He was, indeed, very charming. The other young women fluttered about, glancing admiringly at the impression Amelie had made on her beau. Burke was not sure that his charm would have been enough, but from the moment he entered the room Amelie's eyes were fixed on the despatch case he carried. She clearly guessed what was in it and, with her lover carrying the documents her Empress wanted so badly, his charm was almost superfluous.

Josephine had noticed the case as well and, though she made a good show of disguising her interest, it seemed to Burke that the men who came to petition for her intervention with the Emperor were dealt with more abruptly than on his last visit. It felt hardly any time before Josephine was shooing her ladies out of the room and Burke was again alone with her and Amelie.

Josephine controlled her eagerness enough to go through the ritual of having Amelie pour out tea. She noticed Burke's surprise at the sight of the tea pot and smiled.

"Ah, M de Burgh, don't tell me you are another of those British men who think that the French are too ignorant to make tea. I can assure you it is quite the thing in the afternoon."

As she spoke she took her cup (Empresses naturally being served before mere mortal guests) and started to ladle what seemed to Burke vast quantities of sugar into it. Amelie passed him a cup and a sugar bowl and, in the interests of politeness, he added several spoonfuls of sugar himself. It was a great shame, he thought. He had been excited at the idea of a cup of tea and the pleasure was quite destroyed by the cloying sweetness of the drink. Amelie smiled, though, so he had obviously done the right thing.

Little cakes were produced and politely nibbled at. Actually, Josephine, Burke noticed, did not nibble, but took healthy bites. She was not a greedy woman (in fact she ate very little) so Burke concluded that the stories about her rotten teeth were true and that she was anxious not to display them. By contrast, Amelie did indeed nibble, showing very white, even teeth. Burke thought of those teeth nibbling at him and regretted that, if his plans worked out, he was very unlikely to share her bed again.

The polite preliminaries completed, Burke set down his cup of tea and Josephine, eyes fixed on his despatch case, demanded to know what he had for her.

"Your Highness was looking for an indication of your husband's domestic budget. I think this shows that he is in a position to be generous."

Josephine opened the case and started to look through the papers inside. As she read, she appeared more and more shocked. "Ah, *mon Dieu*. I knew he was spending a lot to make such a great show at court, but I had no idea..." She turned to another sheet. "And he dares to complain that I am extravagant!"

She put the papers to one side. "He must give me a proper allowance for my household at Malmaison. If he spends this much on livery, he can hardly complain that he cannot afford an allowance for my few servants."

"Indeed, your Highness. But if I return to the Conciergerie tonight, I hope I may find even more ammunition for your artillery."

Josephine giggled. "Artillery! *Mais oui*. All the nights I've suffered listening to Napoleon talking about the importance of artillery. Well, now you have provided me with my own weapons and I will show him how powerful a woman can be in battle."

Burke had no doubt that she would. He was glad he was not going to be in Napoleon's position tonight.

"Even so, your Highness, it would surely be wise to see if we can acquire more ammunition for your formidable arsenal."

"But to return to the Conciergerie... Do you not think that you may be taking too much of a risk?"

Little did the Empress know how much of a risk he would be taking that evening.

"It should be safe enough," he lied. "And well worth it if it provides you with the information you need."

Josephine smiled across at Amelie. "You see how brave your man is. I shall turn away so that you may kiss him goodbye and then he must be off. But he will be back again for you soon. And you will both have my eternal gratitude."

Amelie smiled back. Burke could see that she appreciated Josephine's words but was realistic about the likelihood of eternal gratitude. Burke moved towards her and took her in his arms. This, he knew, was likely to be the last time they kissed and, as Josephine turned ostentatiously away, he held her to him with a passion that he realised he had not expected to feel.

He turned to leave the room. He had told himself not to look back, but at the door he could not resist a last glace towards Amelie. She was watching him go, the half-smile on her face belied by a troubled look to her eyes.

CHAPTER 22: Back to the Conciergerie

Burke arrived late at the Conciergerie. He had no intention of searching for any more of Napoleon's domestic accounts. Josephine might be disappointed, but he had already furnished her with enough to negotiate with Napoleon and her divorce settlement was hardly his concern. He hoped that Amelie wouldn't fall out of favour when he failed to return to the Tuileries. She was, he thought, rather a special young woman and he would be sorry if she suffered on his account. Tonight, though, he was an agent of King George and the French could all go hang – even the beautiful ones.

Tonight William accompanied him. He was dressed as a clerk, which was much as he had been before, but with a heavier coat and some ink splattered on his fingers to add verisimilitude. The guards recognised Burke and nodded him through without questioning his right to bring a servant with him.

Burke moved easily through the maze of corridors to the office where the inventories were kept. William was carrying a despatch case with the latest records from Malmaison and he set this down on the table while Burke apologised to the clerk. "… So sorry … detained at the Tuileries … Empress Josephine insisted …" He hated to be an imposition, he said. He would be happy to be left alone as he had been the previous night.

The clerk was happy to agree. Why should he not be? Burke had left the place safe and sound the night before and his remarks about the Tuileries and the Empress established him as a reliable character, even better than the letter of authority he carried. Candles were produced (the light was already dying) and the clerk soon bustled away, happy to have an excuse to leave a few minutes early for the night.

William was carrying a case for his papers and Burke spread several sheets on the desk, to guard against the unlikely prospect of somebody coming into the room. He and William settled down to wait for the other clerks nearby to leave.

Eventually the place grew silent. They allowed, as best Burke could judge, ten minutes to pass before they slipped out of the room and made their way towards the infirmary.

They stopped in one of the deserted passages and William removed a tightly tied bag from one of his coat pockets. He took out a pigeon and, held it above his head while Burke pushed his knife into its breast. A satisfying amount of blood drenched his face.

They hurried on towards the gate. It was earlier than the night before and Burke hoped it was a different guard but, in any case, the last man had never got a good look at his face.

As they arrived, Burke turned to William. "Sorry about this," he said, and swung the back of his hand hard against William's face. William shouted something obscene. The noise brought a guard to the gate. He took one look at William and started to unlock it even before Burke could ask him to.

"Hey, Jean." The man shouted back to the guardroom. "Help this fellow to the infirmary."

Jean emerged into the corridor and took one look at William, blood all over his head, face already beginning to swell, and rushed the two of them down the corridor. "What the hell happened to him?"

"It was a stupid accident. He tripped on some stairs and fell. He smashed his head on the stone. I think he's concussed."

"We'll get him bandaged up and then we'll lie him down. If he's really out of it, the apothecary can bleed him."

William was giving a good impression of a man who was partially concussed. His feet were dragging and it took both James and Jean to help him through the door into the infirmary. As they moved through, Burke kicked the door closed behind him and let go of William. Jean hung firmly onto William to support him, which made it very simple for Burke to take the knife from his boot and stab the guard in the back. The knife slipped between the ribs and into the heart. The man was dead almost immediately.

The apothecary had turned as they entered the room. He froze as Burke killed the guard, apparently struggling to believe what he was seeing. As he opened his mouth to shout, Burke put a finger to his lips and, almost reflexively, he paused. That's when William hit him with a roundhouse blow to the head.

The apothecary fell to the floor. Burke had no trouble finding bandages to tie and gag him with. He wished him no harm. Jean's death had been necessary, but there was no need to add to the bloodshed.

William adjusted the last of the knots as Burke stripped Jean's body. "Just the two guards I reckon," he said.

"Seems likely." Burke was putting on the unfortunate Jean's uniform. The advantage of his having been stabbed in the back was that from the front there was no sign of blood. "I didn't hear any chat behind me and I would have expected that if there had been anyone else there."

He opened the door as William released the apothecary's gag. "You can scream now," he said and, to encourage him he kicked him in the crotch as Burke stepped out of the door.

"*Vite! Vite!*" Burke was not at all sure that he could imitate Jean's voice, but the panicked shout he gave could have been anybody. The other guard appeared at the end of the corridor and Burke vanished back into the infirmary, still yelling for his companion to hurry.

The guard had heard a scream and seen Jean calling for him to join him in dealing with whatever situation had arisen in the infirmary. He ran down the corridor and turned through the door. He had grabbed up a musket and the light caught the bayonet, fixed ready to deal with any recalcitrant prisoners. He probably thought he was prepared for anything but Burke standing behind the door stepped out as he came into the room and slid his wicked knife into his back.

The apothecary's gag was retied and it was William's turn to dress as a French soldier. The coat was a little tight and the trousers were on the short side, but the effect was convincing at a distance.

"Check the patients in here."

William moved from bed to bed. Only half a dozen had men in them and at the last one he looked at he recognised Julien.

The man's eyes were closed but as William, holding the lantern, leaned over him, he woke. His eyes were suddenly wide open as he looked up at what must have seemed the face of one of his guards.

"No! No! I am Julien Lagarde. I am a merchant from Lyons."

"It's alright, Julien. It's me, William." Then, remembering he had never used that name on the trip from Normandy, he corrected himself. "It's Jean Baptiste."

But even then his old companion did not recognise him. He stared up, eyes wide with terror but apparently seeing nothing. "Julien Lagarde," he repeated. "From Lyons."

"Stay with him. I'll check the cells."

The first cell was unoccupied but the second housed one man lying on the floor. Burke threw the bolt on the door but it did not open. It was locked as well as bolted.

He sprinted back to the guardroom. There were the keys, hanging in a bunch on the wall. He scooped them up and ran back to the cells. At the second cell the man was up now but huddled defensively in a far corner.

"It's alright. I'm a friend. I've come to get you out of here."

He tried one key after another. It was only the third or fourth that finally turned the lock. The prisoner was still huddled away from the door, apparently unwilling to trust anybody wearing a French uniform.

Burke left that cell and moved to the next. This housed a woman. Could this ragged creature be Pascale, the young beauty William had described?

"Pascale?"

The girl turned towards the grille in the door, drawing herself up as she did so. She fixed Burke with a look of such disdain he felt compelled to apologise for disturbing her.

"I'm sorry to alarm you, ma'amselle. I am a British agent. I am here to get you out."

She bowed her head in acknowledgement as he unlocked the door and followed him into the corridor.

The next cell was empty but there was a man in the fifth. "Is this one of your companions, ma'amselle?"

Pascale looked through the grille and nodded. "That's Fabrice." There were tears in her eyes. "Poor man."

Fabrice was presumably less seriously injured than Julien, as he had not been sent the infirmary, but he certainly looked in bad shape. His face was a mass of bruises and one eye was swollen closed.

At the sound of Pascale's voice, he had risen to his feet and limped his way towards the door. He moved slowly and was obviously in pain. Burke only hoped that he could manage to walk, because his plan, such as it was, relied on that.

"Julien is in the infirmary. We need to join him."

"What about the fourth in our group? An Englishman, but he called himself Jean Baptiste."

"Don't worry ma'amselle. He's safe and you will see him soon."

Pascale smiled. William, it seemed, had made a conquest.

They opened the door and helped Fabrice out of the cell. He was shoeless and his bare feet showed were bruised and bloody from beating, but with Burke and Pascale supporting him he managed a staggering walk.

As they entered the infirmary, Pascale let out an excited cry at the site of William and ran over to join him. He had got Julien out of bed. "I waved a knife at the geezer in charge" – William indicated the apothecary – "and he said he's alright to be moved. They got carried away and beat him unconscious, but he should be able to walk now."

"I will help him." Pascale, moved to take his arm as if there was no more to be said on the matter.

Burke looked at her, effortlessly taking command, and decided there was, indeed, no more to be said on the matter.

William smiled encouragement at Pascale but when he turned to Burke his face was grim. "I don't like the look of Fabrice. There's you, me and the girl and we have two men who'll need help. Fabrice looks as if he needs somebody to support him on either side but that leaves me helping Julien. You can hardly be commanding an escort if there isn't any bloody escort. It makes it tricky to do your French NCO bit and talk us out of here."

Although he had spoken quietly, Pascale had heard him. "What about the man in the cell next to mine?"

"If you noticed him, then you'll know that he is in no fit state to help us. The poor man's broken. He won't even leave his cell."

"Let me see what I can do."

Pascale vanished away, leaving William to help Julien to walk while Burke struggled to support Fabrice. It was, he soon realised, an impossible task. The poor man struggled to put any weight on his feet. Burke, standing on his left, was able to take the weight on that leg, but every other step took an eternity as Fabrice gently eased the weight onto his right foot, sobbing with the pain of it. Escaping with Fabrice, Burke decided, would be impossible. Yet leaving him to be interrogated by Fouché was impossible too. Burke thought of the knife, safely tucked back into his boot, and what he would have to do with it.

Gently, he sat Fabrice down on his bed and reached toward the knife.

At that moment Pascale returned with the prisoner from the cell next to her own. The man's eyes still darted fearfully from side to but he allowed Pascale to lead him by the hand towards Burke.

"This is Gerard," she said. "He has had a bad time, but he is strong. He will help us."

Gerard was a big man and, it seemed to Burke, strong enough for the job, but there was something about his eyes that suggested he might struggle to understand what was wanted of him. Unlike the other men, he seemed to have nothing wrong with his body but Fouché had somehow destroyed his mind. Still, Burke decided, if he was to get Fabrice out alive, he would have to rely on Gerard.

"Good man, Gerard," he said. "Help me get him on his feet." Burke started to help Fabrice up, but Gerard held back. Burke could see his knuckles whiten as he gripped Pascale's hand, apparently terrified of letting go of the woman.

"Let me," said Pascale. She led Gerard to Fabrice and she started to help him up on her own. Immediately, Gerard released her hand and, taking Fabrice's other arm, lifted him easily.

Pascale gave Burke the glimmer of a smile. "There you are, *monsieur*. Your problem is solved."

Burke nodded his appreciation but his face was grim as he explained what was to happen next.

"We're going to walk out of here. I saw muskets in the guardroom and Sgt Brown and I are your escorts. Brown will be assisting Julien to walk. He'll hold him firmly by the arm and make it look as if he's marching a prisoner out. I will be leading the way. If we are challenged, I will talk us through. The rest of you say nothing."

He vanished back to the guardroom, returning with the muskets. Neither, he noticed, was loaded and, looking at the state of them, he was planning to keep it that way. They looked as if they were left over from before Napoleon had taken control of France. They were good enough for looking smart when an officer came to inspect the guard and the butts would serve as useful clubs if prisoners gave any trouble. If they were loaded, though, there was every chance of them firing the first time a jolt dislodged the aging trigger mechanism or, if they didn't fire prematurely, that they would not fire when you needed them to. No, the muskets were just for show – though the bayonets hanging from the French uniform webbing might well be useful in a fight.

With muskets slung over their shoulders Burke and William gave a convincing impression of a prisoner escort and soon they had their four charges shuffling and shambling back towards the entrance of the Conciergerie. There was an anxious moment when Burke tried all the keys on the ring and was unable to unlock the gate that separated the cells from the rest of the Conciergerie but he found it at last, hanging on a separate hook in the guardroom. He locked the gate behind them and took the key with him. If there was any pursuit, it might delay things a few minutes.

Along the corridor; turn; another corridor; stairs; another corridor.

At this hour they saw almost nobody and those few clerks who were about ducked out of sight. Soldiers escorting prisoners, even this long after the Terror, made people uneasy. Simpler, it seemed, not to be involved.

At one point, Burke was convinced that he had taken a wrong turning but it was just that he was confused by the snail's pace at which they were travelling.

Finally he saw the corridor that led to the entrance. He marched at the front of his little procession with the swagger of a newly promoted NCO enjoying the responsibility of having prisoners under his command.

They were in a hallway just inside the gate which the guards used as a sort of mess room, so the soldiers responsible for guarding the doors were often joined by others who idled there in between carrying out their duties. Burke had hoped that at that hour the place would be virtually empty but there were half a dozen men lounging around. One was a young captain. Burke cursed inwardly. He remembered being a young captain: senior enough to want to be seen to be doing things properly and junior enough not to have learned the advantages of a quiet life.

Sure enough the man was stepping out to block their way. "You!" he said, "What do you think you're doing?"

Burke snapped off a salute. "Prisoner transfer, sir."

"At this time of night?"

"Yes, sir. Citizen Fouché said he has had enough of them and wants them in La Force."

Fouché's name, as Burke expected, had its predictable effect. The officer swallowed nervously and passed them through. At that hour of the night, though, the main entrance, open during the day was sealed with a barred gate and a porter had to open it for them. Burke watched him walk from his bench by the wall to the gate. He carried a keyring on his belt and carefully selected one key from the three or four on the ring. Why, thought Burke, did he have so many keys when he was only responsible for the one gate? And why was he so infernally slow?

Burke was conscious of the men passing their time there turning to look at his little group, which was probably providing the most interest of any of the comings and goings that night.

The gatekeeper removed one key from the ring with the care, it seemed to Burke, of a surgeon teasing a musket ball from a wound. Couldn't he just leave the key on the ring? They seemed to have been standing there forever.

Finally he turned the key in the lock of a postern gate so that they could file out. Slowly, so slowly, the gate was swung open and the six of them moved through into the night. Burke offered up a silent prayer. He had felt the eyes of the men on his back as he had taken the final steps to freedom.

His back! Damn – they had been standing behind him; they must have seen –

As he remembered the bloodied tear on the back of his uniform, he heard a voice behind him. "Captain, there's something wrong ..."

"Go! I'll guard your rear. Go as fast as you can!"

The long, slow walk through the Conciergerie had given Julien time to recover and, though he was hardly in any condition to outrun the guards, he was able to put on a surprising burst of speed. Fabrice, though, could not be expected to run on those horribly damaged feet, even with Gerard and Pascale supporting him.

Burke knew he should use the few seconds he had to kill the agent. It was brutal, but it was the only way to protect the network of houses they had travelled through. In any case, with Fabrice dead, the others might be able to escape.

For a moment, Burke hesitated. Then he was drawing his bayonet and stabbing through the bars of the gate toward the turnkey. The man, predictably, pulled back out of Burke's reach. But in his hurry to avoid the bayonet, he left the key in the lock.

Burke pulled the gate to and, reaching through the bars, locked it and pulled out the key.

Some of the guards had realised what was happening and were running for the gate. Three swords slashed towards him through the bars, but he had stepped back out of reach and was throwing the key out into the darkness.

He had bought them time, but with Fabrice still limping so painfully slowly, their chances of escape must surely still be slim. Then, amazingly, he saw Gerard bend, lift Fabrice, throw him over his shoulder and start to jog off after William with Pascale running alongside him. Perhaps they could still pull this off!

He ran to catch up the others. Behind him there was a confusion of shouted voices. He heard the crack of a musket and a ball chipped stone from the wall.

He slowed and glanced back. Unable to open the postern gate without the key, they had unlocked the main gate. It was heavy and swung open slowly, but the first of the soldiers was already squeezing through. Behind him, another man had a musket raised and was taking aim through the bars.

Burke ran down the steps that led to the street. Ahead of him the others were moving faster, terror driving them on.

There was the sound of a shot behind him and he staggered, almost losing his footing. He had been hit. There was no pain yet – that would come soon enough – but he could see blood staining his trousers at the thigh. He forced himself to keep running, but his leg wouldn't let him move as fast as he needed. The others, for all that they were struggling with Fabrice, were moving away.

He saw William turn and hesitate. Uncertainty flickered across his sergeant's face.

"Do your duty!" he shouted. "Get them out of here!"

William paused an instant before discipline took over and he was running again, herding the prisoners into the shadows of the street.

Burke was running too but, however much he forced himself to ignore the pain, the damage to his leg kept slowing him. Every few steps he staggered. He could hear the crash of boots on the stone steps behind him, horribly close as he broke out into the street after William.

As he followed the others, he heard the sound of a carriage rattling along the cobbles. Turning, he saw a coach pulling away from the side of the road, the driver whipping the horses into a trot.

He should have known, he realised. Fouché, people said, was the devil himself, aware of every plan against Napoleon before the plotters knew their plans themselves. Of course he would have a man in the street with a carriage ready to scoop up any English spy stupid enough to try to break people out of the Conciergerie.

He forced himself to sprint a few more yards, but his efforts had blood pouring from the wound and he swayed, nearly falling.

The coach was alongside him, the coachman pulling at the reins and calling his horses to stop. The door opened and a hand reached out.

"Get in you fool!"

This was not the gruff voice of one of Fouché's thugs. This was a woman.

He grabbed the proffered hand and was pulled into the coach.

"*En y va!*"

The coachman responded with a crack of his whip and they were moving away at a speed that sent jolts of agony through his leg.

"Do try not to bleed on my dress. It's practically new."

He had not imagined it. It was Amelie.

"Fancy meeting you here," he said. She started to smile, but then he noticed the tears in her eyes. He should say something to reassure her.

He began to lift his head to speak but, before he could utter a word, he felt a sudden weariness overwhelming him. Even the pain in his leg was passing away into a fog.

Then nothing.

CHAPTER 23: *La Tour Bonbec*

Fouché had finished writing his reports and made his way to the old torture chamber. The interrogations had been frustrating. In the end, subtlety and all his little psychological tricks had counted for nothing. He had had his guards beat the two men and, if their reports were to be believed, tonight they would tell him all he needed to know.

He took no satisfaction in what was to come. He felt, to tell the truth, disappointed. Disappointed in the stupidity of his prisoners who had suffered unnecessarily – for it had always been inevitable that they would talk eventually – and disappointed in himself for having to resort to brute force to get the truth.

When he arrived in the *Tour Bonbec*, after he had climbed laboriously up the long spiral staircase, he expected to find the prisoners ready for him, but there was no one there, sat in front of the table waiting to make their confession.

It was annoying, but hardly to be surprised at. From what he had been told the prisoners were likely to have trouble walking. His guards would have to struggle to get them up to his chamber. He sat quietly and waited. He was good at waiting.

His leg ached. The limp didn't usually trouble him too much, but the last few days had been trying and he was tired and the walk to the tower had seemed to take it out of him more than usual.

He rested his leg, wondering what could be causing the delay. Was there anything out of the ordinary happening this evening?

Now he came to think of it, there had seemed to be an unusual amount of activity going on in the Conciergerie that night. By this time, the place was ordinarily quiet, but tonight, on his way to the *Tour Bonbec*, he had thought he heard shouts and the sound of running feet. He had even imagined at one point that he might have heard a shot, but that was, of course, impossible. If there was any unrest in Paris that might lead to a shot being fired in the Conciergerie, he would have heard of it.

It was disconcerting, though. He realised that he probably knew more about the mood of the people in the dockyards of Marseilles than he knew of the men who hurried round the Conciergerie every day. It had never occurred to him to take any particular interest in them. Maybe that was a mistake. Tomorrow he would set about placing some of his own agents in the place. It was wrong that his spies should watch everyone but those closest to him.

His thoughts were interrupted by a hesitant knock on the door.

* * *

It was Fouché's boast that he never lost his temper. There was, after all, nothing to be gained by it.

On this occasion he came close enough for him to decide that the best thing was to return home, calm himself, and then find out who was responsible for this disaster and deal with them by the cold light of day.

Later he was to realise what a mistake this was. If he had taken control immediately, closed the bridges, sent patrols throughout Paris, sealed off the insalubrious neighbourhoods where men might go to ground, then he thought he might have stopped them. If he had roused every Royalist sympathiser from their beds and had them thrown into cells all over the city, then he might have heard a whisper of where the prisoners had vanished. But he had left the tasks to other, lesser minds.

And now he had lost them.

CHAPTER 24: Hidden away in Paris

When Burke came to, he was in a bed he did not recognise and somebody was wiping sweat from his brow with a cool cloth.

"You had us worried for a while." Amelie sounded subdued. "The doctor has sewn up your leg. He says it will heal perfectly, but you've lost a lot of blood and you'll need to rest."

Burke grimaced.

"I wish I could. I have to get out of Paris."

"There's no question of that. You're going to have to stay here."

Burke struggled to sit up. He was in a tester bed, the curtains richly embroidered. There were tapestries on the walls and the paper was hand painted.

He fell back against the pillows. Amelie was right: he was in no state to go anywhere.

"You need to get away and leave me. Fouché is after me and, when he finds me, you need to be nowhere near. I don't want you taken down with me."

More sweat had gathered on his forehead with his effort to sit up and Amelie again wiped his face with the cloth. "He won't find you here."

"Amelie, I'm talking about Fouché. He'll find me. He'll find you. You need to run."

She shook her head and gently repeated, "He won't find you here."

"Have we left Paris?"

She laughed. "Hardly. We're in the Tuileries."

"Good God! Are you mad?" Burke tried to sit up again, as Amelie gently but firmly pressed him back down on the bed. "How long was I unconscious? Fouché must already be on his way."

"In answer to your first question, I am not mad. I am distressed that you even consider the possibility." She tried to sound cross, but she was smiling as she spoke. "As to the second: you slept through the night and it is now 11 o'clock in the morning. And before you start to explain that that means you have not a moment to lose – you are in the safest place in France: one where neither Fouché nor any of his servants can penetrate."

She sat waiting for him to ask the obvious question. Burke refused to give her the satisfaction.

After an extended pause, she gave a little pout of irritation and told him anyway.

"You are in the Empress Josephine's apartments."

"What!"

"Hush, *mon cheri*. You are quite safe, but it's perhaps wiser not to shout quite so loudly." She was laughing now. He did love to hear her laugh. For a moment it made him forget the absurdity of what she had just said.

"This is the Empress's bedroom?"

"Oh no." Amelie looked around it slightly disapprovingly. "The tapestries are very inferior. And *He* has his bloody bees all over the wallpaper."

'He' must be Napoleon, Burke decided. The Emperor's personal arms had bees in them and, looking at the wallpaper, Burke did notice bees concealed in the fantastical foliage that separated the vaguely Egyptian images that seemed to be the theme of the piece.

"Josephine's quarters," Amelie explained, "is a little suite of guest rooms, reception rooms, a study, dressing rooms –"

Burke cut her off "Maybe not that little."

"Be that as it may,"-- Amelie's tone suggested that she resented any implication that her Empress was at all extravagant in her taste. "It gives you a safe place to stay. Nobody gets in here without permission except Napoleon. And certainly not Fouché."

"So Josephine knows I am here?"

"Of course."

"Then she must have her suspicions that I'm…" Burke trailed off. He didn't like to say the actual words 'a spy'.

"An agent of the British," Amelie finished for him. There was a short silence, uncomfortable on Burke's part, but apparently not for Amelie, who continued matter-of-factly. "The Empress had her doubts from the beginning. You were just too convenient, suddenly appearing like that and practically boasting of your skills in intrigue. And then you so patently obviously wanted an excuse to visit the Conciergerie. But we weren't sure. Even when you said you would return tonight, although you had already exceeded all her hopes – even then we weren't quite sure. But there was one important detail that you forgot."

"And that was?"

"Your fee. You forgot to negotiate your fee."

"Ah." She was right, of course. It had been a stupid error. He had been careless because he thought of Josephine as a flighty woman with a disreputable past and because Amelie was so pretty it had never occurred to him that she might be clever too.

"What a lot of trouble you women take to make men think you haven't a thought in your head."

"We survived the Terror when most of our menfolk died. We became very good at looking as if we didn't understand politics."

"But if you knew what I was, why did you let me get away with it."

She shrugged. "You got Josephine the information she wanted. And we really weren't sure until tonight."

"But when you saw me at the Conciergerie, you knew."

She nodded. "I knew. And now Josephine knows too."

"So why don't you hand me over? I'm an enemy spy."

Instead of replying immediately she bent over and kissed him.

"You don't feel like an enemy. Why do you think I would feel the English are my enemy?" She sat up straight, her face serious. "Did you know that Josephine was imprisoned during the Terror?" Burke shook his head. "Well, she was. Her husband was guillotined. If Robespierre had not died when he did, Josephine would probably have followed him to the scaffold. If she had had a chance to escape, where do you think she would have gone? To England, where so many of us went."

"Of you?"

"The aristocrats. The public enemies. Everyone that Robespierre and his creatures tried to kill. The men fled and the women stayed with relatives in the country, or with nuns, or they took lovers who had friends who could protect them. And they sewed, and they played the pianoforte, if they were lucky enough to have a pianoforte, and they made bright, cheerful gossip and the men..." She gave a Gallic shrug and gestured with her hands as if throwing something away. "The men just didn't notice we were there." She paused, her face suddenly older. "So when it was all over, we were still alive. We had survived. But those old habits run deep. We laugh and we gossip and we still sew – but, *monsieur*, do not ever think that we are stupid."

Burke thought back to when he had first seen Josephine surrounded by her ladies and thought how much it looked like any other court.

"How many of the Empress's ladies are from the *ancien régime*?"

"Not from the *ancien régime* exactly, but most of us have relatives who suffered under Robespierre. And many of us have family in exile in England."

"So you are happy to work against France."

Amelie coloured. "That's outrageous! We are all loyal to France. I would never betray my country!"

"And yet here I am."

She nodded. "And here you are." She looked at him consideringly. "Do you think that you are a threat to France? Your servant might be – helping those people escape. I assume they were the reason you are here."

Burke nodded. There seemed no point in denying it.

"But I am not concealing them. I am concealing you. And once you are healed, I trust you to get back to England. You're no threat to us in Paris."

He took her hand, raised it to his lips and kissed it. "Thank you. And is that the reason Josephine is hiding me too?"

"Partly. Mainly, though, she hates Fouché. She loves her Napoleon, you know. For all her silly ways, she truly loves him. And she will never forgive Fouché for trying to drive them apart. The man is a treacherous little toad. He was there under Robespierre, he was there under the Directory and now, under Napoleon the wretched creature is still there. They say he is the only man on earth Napoleon is afraid of."

Burke thought of Fouché's reputation as the man who knew the secrets of every French citizen and he realised he could well believe Napoleon feared him. It was too much power to allow any one man to hold.

"So I am here so that Josephine can hurt Fouché?"

Amelie nodded. "Welcome to the world of court intrigue."

* * *

Burke stayed in the Tuileries for ten days. Amelie was an attentive nurse and monitored his progress by the energy he brought to their lovemaking. After a week she thought he was pretty well recovered, but she kept him in bed another three days to be on the safe side.

On the fourth day, though, Amelie was summoned to see the Empress and returned somewhat agitated. James, who had grown to admire the matter-of-fact way that she dealt with an English spy hidden away in the Tuileries, felt the change in her manner could mean no good. Her sudden insistence that he get up and dress was not reassuring either.

A maid brought in new clothes. "We can't have you wandering around the Tuileries in a regular uniform. It would offend the other guards – the ones *He* likes to see dressed up in so much gilt." She didn't mention the holes and the blood, which Burke felt was quite tactful of her.

Amelie fussed over him, tweaking his coat here, straightening his shirt there.

"I think we got your size quite well."

"It's impressive." It really was, Burke thought. Amelie had managed to order clothes almost as well fitted as those the tailor had produced after measuring him up.

"I cheated a little. Some of the women here were able to guess which tailor you had been using. He's very good, but his pocket flaps are always that tiny bit too short. Anyway, he had kept a note of your size. And the pocket flaps are just right. I checked."

"I'm impressed. But why take such trouble now?"

"The Empress wants to see you."

'The Empress', he noticed; not 'Josephine'.

"Is something wrong?"

"No." She hesitated, biting her lip. "Yes."

Fouché, it appeared, was watching the Tuileries.

"He doesn't know you are in here, not for sure. If he did, he would go to the Emperor and denounce Josephine. He can't do that unless he is absolutely certain. But he does have men on all the gates and he has spies among Napoleon's servants."

Burke raised a sceptical eyebrow.

106

"He does!" Amelie's voice was shrill. The mention of Fouché's name struck terror even here in the Tuileries. "He is the devil," she insisted – and Burke was beginning to think she might be right.

"Josephine has to get you out. She risks too much by having you stay here. But I don't know how she plans to do it." She brushed an imagined speck of dirt from his lapel. "Come! We must hurry."

She led him to Josephine's private quarters where they had first hatched the plan to steal Napoleon's papers. In contrast to Amelie, Josephine was the epitome of calm. She smiled as James bowed.

"M de Burgh." Burke straightened and the Empress gave him an appraising look. "I don't suppose your name is de Burgh, but let's carry on calling you that." She gestured to a chair and Burke sat carefully down. It was a delicate piece with finely carved legs and he was worried that he might sit down too hard and snap it. "Amelie, coffee, I think."

Amelie curtsied and vanished out to return, almost immediately, accompanied by a maidservant carrying a tray with a coffeepot and cups for three.

Josephine turned to Burke, "Unless you prefer chocolate?"

It was not really a question. Coffee, he said, would be perfect.

The maid fiddled with the cups, putting them down with a great rattling of china and cutlery. There was a plate of little cakes too and more plates to eat them from and cake forks and –

""Leave us." The maid almost dropped her tray on the table in her hurry to depart. "Amelie, you can take over. Amelie busied herself with the cups and saucers, while Josephine watched Burke, as if assessing how much she could get for him at auction. It was, Burke felt, an uncomfortably direct look and he found himself concentrating on the way Amelie was arranging the chinaware.

The silence stretched out. Amelie poured coffee for the Empress, who took the tiny porcelain cup – Sevres china, Burke could tell, with paintings of camels and pyramids reflecting the Egypt-mania that had followed the French expedition to the Nile. Burke remembered his part in the ultimate failure of Napoleon's efforts in the land of the pharaohs and allowed himself the merest hint of a smile.

Josephine noticed it, of course. She didn't miss much.

"You are amused by the design. You are remembering, perhaps, Nelson's victory on the Nile. Were you there?"

Burke blushed like a schoolboy caught out by a strict governess in some childish misdemeanour.

"I had that honour, your Imperial Highness."

To his surprise, she laughed.

"Poor Napoleon. He hated being bested like that, you know. But somehow he has persuaded everybody that Egypt was a wonderful victory, so now people keep giving him gifts to commemorate his battles. I insist on using this china, just to annoy him." And she laughed again.

Burke couldn't help but smile. Josephine had incredible charm and, even at her age, considerable sex appeal. She could reveal wicked claws and, seconds later, be nothing but a fluffy kitten demanding your adoration. And then she could change again – as she did now.

She put down the coffee cup and was all business.

"I don't know what you have done to annoy M Fouché so much and I do not want to know. You are Amelie's friend and Fouché's enemy and either of these alone would make me inclined to help you. As it is, I find it almost impossible to refuse you assistance. But can you assure me that nothing you will do until your return to England will damage France in any way? You aren't carrying any terrible secrets or planning to assassinate a general on your way home?"

She asked the question lightly, but she watched as he answered and he knew she was serious.

"No, your Highness. My business in France is done. Whether I return to London or not will not affect the outcome of my mission."

"Very well. We must see you on your way. I suppose Amelie has told you that that odious man, Fouché is watching the entrances to the Tuileries?"

"She has."

"So we have to find a way to get you out unseen."

"In a crate?"

"It's not very dignified, is it? Or very practical really. Fouché knows far too much of what goes on in the palace. A crate suddenly being moved out of my apartments – well, it's unusual enough to draw his attention. And while he can't trespass into my private domain, any crate is unlikely to make it for many metres beyond my doors before it is opened."

She was smiling again.

"Tell me, can you drive a carriage?"

* * *

René Voisin had driven the Empress for years. He knew her and her little ways. She would call him by name sometimes as she set off on one of her trips about town and, like so many men, he was a little bit in love with her. Not that he would ever admit that, even to himself. Liberté, égalité and fraternité only went so far and he knew his place. So he was surprised when he was summoned from his room over the carriage house and called to visit the Empress in her private apartments.

He was even more surprised by what he was asked to do when he arrived there.

* * *

Fouché's spies noticed the coachman's visit. It was unusual enough for them to make a note of it. They would have to keep a close watch on him over the next few days in case the Empress was planning to use him in some way. Perhaps he had been given a message to carry out of the Tuileries. His room would be searched and he would be followed whenever he left the palace, but he was just one of dozens of people who were under observation. The watchers' response to the coachman was simply routine. When they saw him make his way directly from Josephine's apartments to oversee the harnessing of the Empress's carriage they imagined she had simply had some instructions about an extra fur in the carriage (the night was chilly) or a question about the condition of the road. In any case, once Voisin had left in the carriage, he was not their concern. There were watchers all over Paris. His movements would be reported on wherever he went.

CHAPTER 25: Malmaison

When James Burke had said that he could drive a carriage, he was thinking of his boyhood in Ireland, driving the little dog cart from his father's house to collect rent from his tenant farmers. Handling the Empress's carriage with its two high-spirited horses was another matter entirely. Despite the chill of the wind he was sweating inside Voisin's greatcoat as he wrestled the reins, trying to keep the carriage steady on the road to Malmaison.

Josephine made the journey regularly and it was not unusual for her to be travelling alone between her apartments in the Tuileries and the house she loved so much outside the city. Burke was glad she knew the route. He had no idea of the road at all and in the dark it was all too easy to take a wrong turn or even just to catch in one of the ruts in the road. He could easily end up with a damaged wheel or, worse, a broken axle and he had no desire to make things easy for Fouché and his men.

Josephine had opened the hatch that enabled passengers to shout instructions to the driver and she was providing a continuous commentary on the route, the state of the road and the quality of Burke's driving. After a while her constant comments and criticisms were driving him mad but he hung on grimly hauling the reins in one direction and the other, terrified that at any moment he might turn the carriage over. Inside he heard Josephine laugh. She was enjoying the ride far too much.

After what seemed an eternity, but was probably less than a couple of hours, they crunched over the gravel of the drive that led to Josephine's private home, Malmaison. Flambeaux either side of the entrance threw enough light for Burke to see that, however humble its name, Malmaison was a substantial building of three floors with two wings extending either side of the main block with high gabled roofs at the end giving almost the appearance of towers.

Servants ran from the entrance to hold the horses, and bring steps to the carriage so that as the door was opened the Empress could descend elegantly and safely – her safety doubly assured by the footman who offered an arm to grasp as she stepped down.

She paused as she drew level with the front of the carriage and called up to James.

"Voisin, leave the grooms to take the carriage. You come in with me."

* * *

110

They walked along corridors of parquet covered in oriental runners and then she opened a door to a bedroom.

Burke made a slight bow of appreciation but said that he could not afford to rest. "I need to be on my way before Fouché's jackals pick up my scent. It's best I travel by night."

Josephine patted the bed.

"Stop fussing and sit down."

Burke hesitated. This was the Empress. Did he have a choice?

Josephine patted the bed again, but the imperious tone was slipping as she spoke.

"It will be hours yet before they realise you have slipped their net. Quite possibly days. And you need to rest. You have been injured. I must be your nurse and insist you lie down, at least for a few hours. You can leave before dawn if you want."

"What if this place is watched as well?"

Her eyes crinkled in amusement. "Of course it's watched, silly. Only not very well. I trust my servants – well, almost all of them and the ones I don't trust are watched in their turn by the ones I do. M Fouché –" she spat the name "– has one or two men lurk about the place, but we are quiet round here and strangers are conspicuous. I can always be confident of knowing exactly where they are."

The bedroom was at the back of the house and she threw open French windows that led out into a garden, beautiful in the moonlight. Burke could have sworn he heard a lion roar nearby.

"The grounds here are far too big for a couple of Fouché's thugs to watch. I'm surprised you haven't heard of them. I suppose your check of the inventories never got as far as the zoo."

He was right. That was a lion's roar he heard.

"You're much better off staying until there's a glimmer of light. I'll have someone show you the safest way to leave. There will be a horse ready for you. And you are safer by daylight – less likely to get lost and less likely to be noticed too."

James hesitated. There was something in what she said after all.

He heard the lion again.

Josephine pouted. "It would be a shame if you wandered round the garden in the night and got eaten by something."

The lion's cries were joined by something else that growled menacingly.

Josephine closed the French windows. It occurred to James that the menagerie outside was as effective a prison guard as any.

"Is it so much to ask that you spend a few hours with me?"

The coquettishness had gone, as had the earlier imperiousness. Now there was just a woman who, James realised, very much needed a friend. When Napoleon had met her she had been one of the most desirable women in Paris. He had raised her up and made her his Empress – one of the most powerful women in the world. Now, though her charms were still considerable, they were beginning to fade and Napoleon was about to cast her aside as his consort.

He crossed the room and took her in his arms.

"I will spend as long as you want."

For a moment she clung to him. Then, as if recalling herself, she took a step back. She held him at arm's length, looking into his face. It seemed to Burke that she was searching for something. "It's ironic, isn't it," she said, "that I should turn for a friend to someone whose country seeks to destroy all that I hold dear."

"War makes strange companions. I do not choose my country's enemies, but I can choose my friends."

Josephine gave a smile but her lips were trembling. James worried she might start to cry. How do you comfort a weeping Empress?

"I love him, you know. People say I am hard and greedy and do not care for him, but I do. And Fouché and all those others with their sneers about my past – they will take him from me. And they will lead him to his death. I can feel it. I can feel it in my soul. And it hurts."

The way you comfort a weeping Empress, Burke discovered, is much the way you comfort anyone else. You hold them and you listen.

So Burke listened while this legendary beauty poured out her fears and her doubts; her worries about her future and the future of the man she loved.

Eventually, she slept.

For a while he lay holding her, thinking about all that she had said. She had revealed things about Napoleon that his masters in London would give much to know, but he would never tell them.

Eventually he, too, fell asleep.

When he woke, it was morning, and Josephine was gone.

CHAPTER 26: On the Road

He need not have worried about the menagerie. The animals were all safely caged, except for some peacocks whose cacophonous cries had wakened him at dawn. A suit of travelling clothes and a pair of handsome riding boots had been laid out for him. A purse that held more than enough travelling money and a neat little book that folded out into a map of France were set alongside the clothes. A maid had brought in a bowl of hot water and shaving kit and, ten minutes later, a silent manservant had guided him through Malmaison's huge gardens, the grass glistening under an early frost, until they arrived at a discreet gate almost hidden behind a hedge. Beyond the gate a groom waited with a stallion pawing at the ground, its breath steaming in the morning air.

Burke mounted and the groom gave him a supercilious look, which he thought unbecoming in a servant. "The Empress," the man said, "has asked me to inform you that England is in that direction," and he gestured vaguely toward the horizon before turning abruptly and vanishing back into Malmaison's grounds.

Burke wasted no time in following the Empress's advice and headed to the north-west. Fouché, he was sure, would learn soon enough that Burke had fled the Tuileries and would be on his trail. He hoped that William and the others had made it clear of Paris as well, but on the first day the important thing was to get as far from the capital as possible.

He had not worked out his route in detail. For now it was sufficient to put a goodly number of miles between himself and Paris. He would then head directly towards Normandy. He wouldn't try to back-track along the way that William had taken on his journey from the coast, for they had taken a circuitous path to avoid detection and Burke just wanted to get to Petit-Caux as fast as he could. Malmaison was not far from the Seine and he thought he could follow along the river and then take any main road north-west.

What he had neglected to consider was that the authorities were on heightened alert because of the escape of William and the others. The first inkling he had of this was at Bougival, barely ten minutes ride from Malmaison. Bougival was near a crossing point of the river, so an obvious place for a checkpoint, but he had imagined that a respectably dressed man on a fine horse would not excite suspicion. When he was stopped by two guards at the crossroads in the centre of the town he was surprised, but unconcerned. They would stop him for form's sake, ask him his business and then let him on his way.

It turned out very differently from that. What was his name? M de Burgh.

Could he show a passport? Surely he did not need a passport.

Technically no, they agreed. But some evidence that he was who he claimed to be would be useful. There were some dangerous people on the road.

Burke cursed inwardly. He did indeed have papers that showed him to be M de Burgh: forgeries, of course, but very good forgeries. The trouble was that they had been abandoned with the rest of his possessions when Amelie rescued him. They were waiting in a hotel room that was almost certainly watched by Fouché's men. There was no way Amelie – or anybody else – could have recovered them.

"I am hardly 'on the road', as you put it." He adopted the privileged accent of those he had met around Josephine's circle. "I was riding out early to exercise my horse and I have travelled rather further from Paris than I had originally intended. In the circumstances, it is hardly surprising that I am not carrying any papers."

The two guards looked at each other. One was a heavy jowled fellow who looked as if he would be happier wielding a pitchfork than the musket he carried. His expression suggested that Burke's tone had not been appreciated. The other man was younger and simply shrugged.

"Probably best if you head back then."

"Very well." Burke, seething inwardly, gave a cheery wave and turned his horse back the way he had come.

His journey, it seemed, would not be straightforward at all.

He rode east, back towards Paris, until he was sure that he was out of sight of Bougival before stopping and consulting the map. It turned out to be of limited use. Certainly it showed all the major towns and quite a few smaller ones as well as the roads connecting them, but these were exactly the places he could expect to find checkpoints or patrols. What he needed was details of the small roads that linked villages and hamlets where he was unlikely to run into any of Fouché's minions.

In the absence of a more detailed map, all he could do was take whatever side roads offered and, guided only by the sun and a strong sense of direction, attempt to shadow the highways that he did not dare to travel on. Suddenly the Alien Office and its elaborate trail of safe houses seemed a lot more sensible than he had given it credit for.

He found a side road soon enough, leading off to the south. It wasn't the direction that would eventually take him to Normandy, but any roads to the north would lead to the Seine and the crossing points would be almost certain to be guarded. South it was then – but this road meandered south for miles with no apparent way to get back on course westwards. By noon he was more than happy to stop for lunch at the first inn he had seen on the road.

After the luxury of meals in Paris the chicken stew was a disappointment. It seemed mainly root vegetables with just the odd scrap of meat: a dispiriting reminder that the loss of men to the war effort was leaving farmers in small places like this struggling. The *patron* was friendly enough, though, explaining that anyone wanting to travel westward would have to go through the property of the Vicomte Morel de Vindé.

"Le Vicomte?"

"Ah, *m'sieur*, he does not use the title, but that is what we call him, who have known him since before the revolution. But he takes no part in politics. He is a scientist and has written much about agriculture." He gave a typically Gallic shrug and gestured towards the stew. "Perhaps when he has written another book, we will be able to grow more food with all our young men still away."

The *patron*'s cynicism, it seemed to Burke, was directed more at the politicians who had conscripted the farmhands into the army, rather than at the Vicomte. The old aristocrat sounded an interesting fellow but Burke felt that this was not the time to be making social calls.

"Are there any paths I could take across his land?"

The *patron* pursed his lips. "I suppose it's possible, but the Vicomte is nervous of strangers on his property."

Burke smiled reassuringly. "It's all right. He'll never know I was there."

The *patron* was obviously uncomfortable with the idea but he wanted to be helpful. There was a path, he admitted: just beyond the village, across a stream by the old stone cross... He gave more details and Burke set off half an hour later, rested, fed and confident that he would soon be back on course towards home.

The path was narrow and not at all obvious, but the directions he had been given were clear enough and soon Burke found himself riding easily through the woods that formed part of the Vicomte's estate. After a couple of miles, though, the path was blocked by a fallen tree at a point where thick vegetation either side made it impossible to force a way past. In fact, the path there was so narrow that even turning his horse to go back was not easy.

Afterwards Burke cursed his carelessness. The situation had all the attributes of an ambush. It was just that the idea of an ambush in the peace of the French countryside had simply never occurred to him. As it was, when a man appeared from the undergrowth and pointed a musket firmly at Burke's chest, it came as a shock.

The man did not look to Burke like a robber. He was respectably dressed with hat and coat and his expression was one of righteous indignation rather than that of a villain and, indeed, his first words suggested that he had every right to be there but doubted that Burke did.

"What do you think you're doing here?"

Burke decided that nothing was to be gained by argument and went instead for a diplomatic approach. "I'm so sorry. I was lost and trying to regain the road west."

The musket never wavered. "Does this look like the road?"

Burke admitted that it did not, but that he had seen no other paths headed in the direction he wanted.

"And which direction do you want?"

"I was heading toward Rouen."

"That's a fair way."

Burke admitted that it was.

"I'd expect anyone going to Rouen to keep to the highways."

"I got lost."

The man gave Burke a hard stare. The lie was so obvious that it was not worth calling out.

"Give me one good reason not to shoot you right now."

Burke was honestly shocked. "You would shoot me down? An unarmed man?" (His knife had survived his adventures and was, as usual, tucked into his boot, but he felt that "unarmed" was close enough to the truth.) "For taking a short-cut through a wood?"

"Do you know whose wood it is?"

"I was told in the village. It belongs to the Vicomte Morel de Vindé."

"Then you should know that this is a man who has to be careful of his life. During the Terror, they came here to execute him, but we hid him safely away and said we did not know where he could be found. Since then he has lived quietly and, importantly monsieur, away from society. Especially the society of Paris." He looked at Burke's fashionable clothes. "You are from Paris, are you not?"

"I am from Rouen."

"But you started your journey from Paris."

Burke admitted that this was true.

"There is a good road from Paris to Rouen. Why did you not take it?"

When all else fails, Burke thought, sometimes it's worth trying telling the truth.

"I had a problem with my papers." The man's face was impassive but Burke noted that his finger was still on the musket's trigger. "I don't have any."

There was a long silence while Burke waited for the man to decide his fate.

Finally: "I think, perhaps, these are waters too deep for me. I will take you to le Vicomte and he must decide what to do with you."

Burke was ordered to dismount and the reins were loosely tied around his hands. With the musket still clearly in evidence, this was all the restraint that was needed.

The man pushed aside a branch and revealed a narrow path leading away from the track. Seeing the expression on Burke's face, he gave a grim smile. "We have our own ways to move through the woods. As soon as you were seen crossing the stream, word was sent and I was on my way to intercept you. Le Vicomte has many friends hereabouts."

They walked for twenty minutes or more before emerging onto an open lawn which surrounded a splendid chateau. Huge and imposing, with its grand entrance and its corner turrets, it seemed to Burke an incongruous palace to find in the middle of nowhere. But then again, it was less than twenty miles from Paris and the land seemed to be good. It made sense that Morel de Vindé was rich and not all aristocrats wanted to show off their wealth. Presumably his taste for living in relative obscurity was the reason his head was still attached to his shoulders.

They ignored the grand entrance and Burke was prodded towards a side door. Three men emerged to meet him. One led the horse away while the other two fell in beside him as he was escorted into the house.

116

It seemed they were in the service quarters – lots of small rooms leading off stone-flagged corridors with cooking smells suggesting they weren't far from the kitchens. It was all clean and tidy and to Burke it gave the impression of a well-run house. He saw nobody in the corridors, but the sound of footsteps from nearby suggested plenty of servants.

His escort drew up outside an anonymous door which opened to reveal a well-furnished office. Burke felt that the precision with which the whole operation was conducted suggested that these men had served in the army and were delivering him to this room as a prisoner might be delivered to be questioned by a senior officer. The man sitting behind the desk (mahogany, Burke thought) wore no uniform, though – unless the formal clothes of a rather superior butler counted as a uniform.

"Your report, Jacques."

Burke's captor gave a succinct account of how Burke had been captured and his explanation of what he was doing there. The butler listened in silence before dismissing him.

Burke was glad to see the musket leave the room but the two who had met him at the door remained and they gave the impression of being more than able to take care of themselves in a fight.

The butler steepled his fingers and leaned forward on his desk, examining Burke in silence for a disconcerting couple of minutes. Burke tried to remain relaxed under his gaze, but he was relieved when the silence was eventually broken.

"Would you like to tell me the truth?"

Burke returned the butler's gaze. The Vicomte's men, it seemed, were no fools. This was a well-organised household run, as far as he could tell, with military efficiency. They would not be fobbed off with some nonsense about losing his way and he was not sure that they would believe anything he came up with about visiting relatives in Rouen. It seemed unlikely, though, that they were sympathetic to the likes of Fouché and his men. He decided that the truth was his best bet.

As he explained, he could feel the atmosphere in the room relax.

"Would your story have anything to do with reports of some prisoners escaping from the Conciergerie a couple of weeks ago?"

"You know about that?"

"Indeed. Word has spread. Fouché is said to be furious. Several guards are enjoying the hospitality of their own cells while his investigations continue." He chuckled. "I understand they may continue for some time."

"I was there, but I was wounded. Did the others make it away?"

He shook his head gently. "I don't know. There are rumours of course. There are always rumours. But I really don't know anything except that Fouché's brutes haven't caught them because we'd be sure to be told about it if they had. So the odds are on their side."

The look of relief on Burke's face was so marked that the butler went on: "I take it you are working for the British."

There seemed little point in denying it.

"And now you're trying to make your way back to the Channel."

"It seemed wiser to say Rouen."

"Just so."

He unsteepled his hands and paused in thought, his fingers tapping on the desk.

"Gilles, Bertrand, stay with our guest. I must consult with M Le Vicomte."

The butler left Burke with his two – he was not sure what they were. Guards? Hosts? They had relaxed to the point where he thought he might be able to draw the knife from his boot and disable them both, but to what end? The house was full of other servants; his horse was stabled away somewhere; he had no real idea where he was going. Best to wait and see what the Vicomte had to say.

He was not kept waiting long. The butler returned in a few minutes and beckoned Burke to follow him. Gilles and Bertrand rose to their feet but the butler waved them away. "I am sure our guest will not do anything to embarrass us all." He turned to Burke. "Do I have your word on that?"

Burke nodded.

"Good. I am to present you to M Le Vicomte. But I am afraid I have neglected to ask you your name." There was the briefest pause and the butler smiled. "I understand your difficulty. A nom de guerre will suffice."

Burke smiled back. "My papers, before they were lost, were in the name of M de Burgh."

While they talked they had moved from the stone flagged corridors into hallways of wood with carpets scattered here and there. They passed through three rooms of increasing splendour before the butler paused at an imposing pair of double doors and knocked. He did not wait for a response but opened one door and, gesturing Burke through, announced him as M de Burgh.

Burke had thought of Morel de Vindé as an old man, based on nothing but his prejudices about the *ancien régime* who he imagined as elderly and out of touch. The Vicomte de Vindé, though, was a good looking man in his forties whose face radiated intelligence. Burke knew that extremely stupid people could be gifted with intelligent faces, but he was prepared to give de Vindé the benefit of the doubt.

There was a desk scattered with papers against one wall of the room, but the Vicomte was seated in an armchair near the window with views out over the lawn and into the woods beyond. As Burke entered he came to his feet and advanced to meet him, hand outstretched.

"M de Burgh, I am delighted to make your acquaintance. I understand you have been thrown here by chance but that we may share many common interests."

"I fear, my lord, that I lack your advantages. I'm told you are an agronomist, but I know nothing about farming. We may, however, share other interests."

118

De Vindé smiled. "You are, I see, not one for small talk. Very well, let us waste no time in idle chatter and instead discuss your recent activities in Paris."

Burke acknowledged the Vicomte's directness with a polite nod before explaining that he had been involved in engineering the escape of some of Fouché's prisoners from the Conciergerie. He called them 'French patriots', which he could see went down well with de Vindé.

"Patriots or not," said de Vindé, "I take it that they are on their way back to England."

"I honestly don't know, my lord. They escaped in the company of a companion of mine who will definitely be heading back to his own country. The others are in no position to continue with their missions, so they may well choose to return with him, but they are free to stay in France should they so wish."

"And what missions were they charged with?"

"There was a young lady, my lord, who I believe was mostly concerned with the distribution of pamphlets attacking the Emperor. The others were military men."

"They were to liaise with dissident elements within our army?"

"I think, sir, that they were to act independently."

The Vicomte's lip curled. "You mean they were to build some sort of infernal machine."

Burke sympathised with de Vindé's distaste for bombing. The Alien Office had been enthusiasts for these 'infernal machines' ever since one had come so close to killing Bonaparte in 1800. Bonaparte had survived but several houses had been destroyed and there had been around a dozen bystanders killed, including a 14 year-old girl. Since then, it seemed to Burke, Fouché's efforts meant that killing Napoleon was getting steadily more difficult and that future bombs would mainly have the effect of killing civilians.

"I cannot say, my lord. I can assure you, though, that my companion and I were not involved in any such plot."

The Vicomte shook his head sadly. "I can hardly believe that the world has come to such a point that men will hide an infernal machine in a street and excuse their cowardice on the grounds of political necessity." He sighed and looked up at Burke. "But if I have your assurance that you were not party to any such plot, then it might be possible to help you."

The Vicomte's plan was essentially similar to the Alien Office's. Burke was to be moved from one sympathetic house to another. "I can't guarantee that we can get you all the way to the Channel, but I think we can be sure of moving you sufficiently distant from Paris to be at little immediate danger from Fouché's agents."

He was, de Vindé said, to start at once. "I am undoubtedly being watched, so the sooner you are on your way, the better for both of us." He was to have the luxury of travelling in a coach for at least the first stage. "We'll dress you in my coat and hat and anyone watching will believe it is me. You are, I admit, younger and some might say handsomer than me, but if you allow yourself to worry about what

Fouché has planned for you, I am sure you will look haggard enough to deceive. More practically, you might take care to sit well back in the seat and rely on the shadows."

So it was decided. The Vicomte, like all good commanders, made a plan, communicated it, and then expected it to be carried out. There was no further discussion.

Burke, in truth, could think of nothing sensible he could add. At least de Vindé had the good sense to travel by day. The Alien Office's obsession with moving by night had, in Burke's opinion, nothing to recommend it. He had always been a great believer in hiding in plain sight.

His journey took him a week. Sometimes he rode, but generally he travelled by coach. Every night he ate well and slept in clean sheets on soft mattresses. His hosts were invariably courteous and none asked for any detail as to what exactly was the nature of his business.

When he reached Fallencourt, only fifteen miles or so from the sea, he asked if he could be given a horse to continue alone. He intended to find the cottage where William had come ashore and he did not want even the men who had helped him to know exactly where he was headed. His host, a soldier in Louis' army, now reduced to the life of a country gentleman, was happy to oblige him – the more so as the countryside near the coast was crawling with troops. "They say they are looking for a very dangerous man who tweaked the nose of Fouché himself and who is now trying to escape to England. I'm sure I can't imagine that such a terrible criminal might be found in our quiet little part of the world." And he laughed so hard he nearly choked on his wine.

Burke set off the following afternoon. For once he agreed with the logic of the Alien Office: if the country was thick with soldiers, he wanted to be moving at dusk when it was easier to merge into the scenery. He remembered that the country was well-wooded. He would ride along the edges of the trees until he was near the farmhouse where William had spent his first night. Then he would head straight across the open farmland at a sharp trot, like a man who was anxious to be home before dark. Nothing, he knew, could be entirely safe, but this was as good a plan as he could come up with and it had, he thought, every chance of success.

The problem with a plan that has every chance of success is that there is always the chance of failure. He did well: he slipped between the trees when he heard a cavalry patrol heading across the open land paralleling the distant coast. He wondered idly if these were the same troopers whose stables he had burned down and if they had found new accommodation. He moved carefully across the few tracks that emerged from the woods, listening for any sign of guards placed to intercept travellers heading towards the sea. Once he heard voices in the dusk and the evening light glinted on the metal of musket barrels. He dismounted and led his horse in a loop around the soldiers, riding on only when he was a good half mile away.

It was his bad luck that the last section of the woods was being guarded by *voltigeurs*, French skirmishers whose officer had decided that, rather than guard fixed piquets, they should practice their skills of concealment, scattered in ones and twos among the trees.

The first he saw of the man who stopped him was when he rose from the scrub ahead of him and levelled a musket at his chest.

He would have run him down – his horse had obviously been trained to battle and would have charged ahead without hesitation, but the man's shout had brought more soldiers to their feet and Burke found himself surrounded by a dozen men, their weapons pointed towards him, their fingers on the triggers.

He dropped the reins and raised his hands in the air. Across the open land beyond the wood he could see a light shining from the farmhouse window. It was less than a mile away.

It may as well have been on the moon.

CHAPTER 27: William's journey home

When William saw Burke hit, it took all his self-control not to run back, but when the major ordered him to save the agents, he knew it was the right thing to do. Getting the three of them out of Fouché's grasp before they could be tortured into betraying the safe houses on their route – that was what the whole mission had been about. So close to success, he could not hesitate now.

Behind them there were shots and confusion. The guards were concentrating on Burke rather than them, giving them vital seconds to get off the main road and start zig-zagging through the alleys of the Île de la Cité.

Pascale and Julien were running fast, fear lending wings to their feet. Gerard, with Fabrice over his shoulder, kept up a steady trot. William could hardly believe the strength of the man.

They had left the immediate danger of pursuit behind them, but they needed to get off the island before anyone thought to seal off the bridges. But where to go then?

They headed across a bridge to the Right Bank. They needed a safe house where a disreputable collection like themselves might not attract that much notice. Fortunately, William knew the very place.

While James Burke had been associating with High Society, William had been spending his evenings with soldiers and other less salubrious sorts. There had been drinking of course – quite a lot of drinking in fact. And then the evening would finish with that other great entertainment of the working man – a visit to a brothel.

They had usually ended up at the Fleur Rouge in the Beaubourg Quartier, conveniently close to the Île de la Cité. William glanced at Pascale and felt himself blush. This, though, was not the time to be embarrassed.

"I'll take you in. You have to look like you're an ..." He hesitated. "An acquaintance."

"A lady of the night," she replied, with a smile. She seemed considerably less embarrassed than he was. The woman never ceased to amaze him.

The Fleur Rouge was watched of course. Everywhere was watched in Fouché's Paris. But all the watchers saw was a drunk taking some raggedy street girl into one of the many legal brothels in the city. He shouldn't have been allowed to take in his own entertainment – these things were supposed to be regulated after all – but it happened. A while later three customers turned up – one big man and one regular fellow supporting a third who was already so far gone in drink that he seemed barely able to stand.

They made a note – they made a note of everything – but nobody ever connected these everyday comings and goings with the escape from the Conciergerie.

Inside the Fleur Rouge William had taken the madam on one side and explained his predicament. Fortunately he had proved a popular customer in the short time he had spent there, spreading Colonel Gordon's gold liberally around the house. Fortunately, too, the house had flourished under the Bourbons and the Fleur Rouge was no friend of Bonaparte. It helped, of course, that William was able to slip away later that evening, lost in a raucous group of other customers, and when he returned the next day he had with him the last of their gold reserves. They had been hidden safely away in the hotel room where Burke's absence had, given the number of nights he had stayed away, yet to draw any attention. While he was out, William had also paid a visit to the livery stables where he had paid his bill, tipped generously, and made arrangements for the rest of their stay.

The next few days passed pleasantly enough at the Fleur Rouge. Pascale kept discreetly to her room but William was somehow always aware of her presence and remained unusually abstemious. As to the others in his little party, he took care not to pay any attention to how they spent their time. He saw Fabrice at meals (the Fleur Rouge kept a good table) and noticed that he was walking better and that was all he cared about. Otherwise he spent his time listening to the girls. The Fleur Rouge liked to think of itself as one of the better class of establishments. William had his doubts about that but it was certainly the case that the madam liked her girls to be well spoken. William's French might pass in rough company but he took this opportunity to work on sounding what the girls assured him was "respectable". Major Burke had always insisted that being able to speak like a native was a key skill for any agent so William decided that it was the best use of his time. It had, he convinced himself, nothing to do with impressing Pascale. In any case, the girls were good company and the stories that he listened to in what he thought of as his language lessons were educational in more ways than one.

As with so many things in France, the operation of the brothels was surrounded with bureaucratic regulations. No other country, William suspected, could be so enthusiastic in its pursuit of sexual pleasure and provide so many detailed rules to make the whole business unnecessarily complicated. The rule that was complicating his life now stated that prostitutes were only allowed to leave the house on specific days, when they were to be accompanied by the madam. The first such day was almost a week off. A week, though, seemed to be needed for the madam to make all the arrangements required. It was to be a high holiday for the girls. Carriages were to be hired. A picnic was to be prepared and everybody would eat in the countryside outside Paris. It might be cold (they were well into autumn by now) in which case they would eat at an inn, but madam hoped that it would be a celebration of the very last of summer. Nervous eyes were kept on the weather.

In the end, it was a lovely day, sunny and bright. There was a touch of chill in the air, but the girls had cloaks and there would be wine to keep everybody warm and spirit burners to make hot cups of coffee.

They made quite a procession – half a dozen carriages rattling down the street. Pascale was dressed for the occasion in clothes every bit as bright as those worn by the ladies who worked at the Fleur Rouge. It was far from her usual fashionable wear but she leaned out of the windows with the rest, waving enthusiastically and blowing indiscriminate kisses at any passing men. She waved particularly enthusiastically at the two men who were trying to look inconspicuous in a nearby doorway and who the other girls pointed out to her as Fouché's lackeys

Three of the ladies were dressed less gaudily and stayed quietly back from the windows. William adjusted his ribboned bonnet. Nobody must ever know about this. Looking at the expressions of Julien and Fabrice, he was confident that they, too, had no intention of ever revealing the way they escaped Paris.

Gerard had remained at the brothel. The Fleur Rouge needed a doorman – someone who could deal with the occasional rowdy customer. Gerard's build made him intimidating enough to be able to stop most trouble simply by looming over any malefactor until they decided that they perhaps urgently wanted to be somewhere else. The girls saw the kind and generous man under the thuggish exterior and adored him. He could live happily at the Fleur Rouge until the fuss had died down. William suspected he might carry on living there even afterwards.

They arrived at the spot selected for the picnic and, amidst much laughter from the girls, the men changed back into their clothes. Pascale shed the most outrageous scarves and ribbons though William could have sworn he saw a look of regret as she parted with them. Two grooms from the livery stables had arrived with the horses they had ridden to Paris and two more for the others in the party. The girls raised their glasses in a toast and cheered as they put their heels to their horses' flanks and set off towards England.

* * *

They made good time, retracing their steps along the chain of safe houses. William knew that, for now at least, they remained secure. Fouché seemed to be still looking for them in Paris. In any case, they saw no reward notices featuring their faces and no additional checks on the roads they took. Even so, they travelled mainly by night and their guides took care to avoid any paths they thought might be watched.

A week later they arrived at the farm where they had spent their first night in France. The second night after they arrived, the Alien Office's agents moved, under cover of darkness, to the cottage near the cliffs. They were to sail on the tide, soon after midnight. William shook hands with Fabrice and Julien and the two men turned and left him alone for a moment with Pascale. She took his hand, holding it a moment more than was strictly proper and looking at him as if he was something strange and wonderful. And then she stretched up and kissed him on the lips.

She saw the shock on his face and laughed – that little laugh he had grown to know so well as they travelled together.

"Did you never even think it?" And she shook her head in wonder.

And William realised he never had. She was a lady and far beyond him. William knew his limits. He and Molly had been married less than a year and he had been away in Spain most of that time, but they were as comfortable together as any old married couple. Pascale was a glimpse of a magical world that might shine brightly but not for long. They both knew that one day she would meet Fouché again and there would be no-one to save her that time.

He reached out and held her to him. He could feel her heart thumping.

"I suppose there's no point in telling you to take care, is there?"

She didn't say anything, but he heard that laugh for the last time and then she was gone with the others.

* * *

Nobody suggested that William might leave with them. It was simply understood that, until word came that the major was dead, William would remain at the farmhouse and wait for him.

Not that waiting came easily to William Brown. Every morning he would ask if there was any news and every morning he would be told that there was nothing in the papers from Paris, nothing in the gossip in the neighbourhood, no messages travelling along the safe houses to be sent back to England.

Gradually he noticed more patrols on the road. Neighbours complained that they were stopped as they went about their business and questioned if they went anywhere near the coast. This had to be, he thought, good news. It looked as if Fouché had failed to take Burke and was determined to stop him from making it back to England.

After a week of being asked for news, his host's nerves snapped. "How would I know what Fouché and his men are up to? If you want any news, you need to ask them yourself."

It was said in a moment of irritation and apologised for almost immediately, but it had set William thinking. Did anybody know how the local forces received their news from Paris? His host promised to ask around.

It took only a few days for him to come back with the news. One of Fouché's agents would ride up a couple of times a week – more often if there was trouble. "There are messengers arriving every couple of days now. I imagined things would have died down by now. They must have realised you slipped the net a while ago. All this excitement suggests that they don't want to make the same mistake with your friend."

They would usually arrive mid-morning and stop at a local inn to eat. "They could eat down at the barracks, of course, but they say the food there isn't fit for pigs." Then they would ride on to the barracks at Dieppe to deliver their despatches. "They usually hang around for the rest of the day, poking their noses in and irritating people. They write their own report that is added to anything they've been given by their chaps here and they ride back the following morning."

"Are they uniformed?"

"No." His host was dismissive. "You know these secret police types. Like to think they are all mysterious – as if we didn't all know what they are up to."

William mulled over what he had been told and came up with a plan. It was so ridiculous that he thought it over for a couple of days before deciding to put it into execution. The inactivity of sitting around the farmhouse was driving him mad – especially as they had just been joined by another party of agents who were due to be taken off by boat later in the week. Everybody, it seemed, was busy in the war against Napoleon while he was doing nothing. His plan would at least give him some sense that he was doing something useful.

The owners of 'The Little Pig' – famous for its food – were allies. An inn near the coast always has close ties with the smuggling community and the government's efforts to stop English boats running ashore had made no friends in the area. When Fouché's messenger next visited the inn a boy was sent running to tell William.

By the time William arrived, the messenger was already dead.

"I fed him mushrooms in the stew," said the *patron*. "I picked them myself. I can't believe I accidentally put in some poisoned ones."

William agreed that it was a tragedy. "I'd better get rid of the body for you. We wouldn't want word getting around that any of your customers had problems with food poisoning."

He slung the body over the messenger's own horse and rode off into the woods. There was no time to bury it, but he left it under a pile of leaves far enough from any track for it to go unnoticed. There weren't many wolves in the region, but there were enough. The body would vanish before long.

He read quickly through the despatches. There were orders to increase patrols along the cliffs. Some people – his host among them – were to be questioned and their homes searched. That order, conveniently on a separate sheet of paper, was soon a few scraps lost among the trees. The only point of interest was that there was a rough description of a fugitive believed to have been seen west of Paris and probably heading towards the coast. He was English but could pass for French and was described as "very dangerous". Well, thought William, they got that bit right. Major Burke was safe for now.

There were details of what was to be done if the fugitive was captured. He should not be killed but must be sent at once with a heavy guard to Paris. A courier was to ride ahead with news of the capture. William grinned. He was happier than he had been since Pascale left. Their exploits at the Conciergerie seemed to be pre-occupying Fouché.

He grinned again.

That was all he had intended to do: kill the courier and read the latest despatches from Fouché's office. It was a tiny blow struck against Fouché's secret police and it reassured him that Burke was still alive and apparently heading towards the coast.

To be honest, he had rather hoped for more information. Fouché's reputation for knowing everything that was going on in France had led him to expect a detailed account of Burke's flight, news of where he had hidden all this time and, crucially, when he might be expected to turn up in Normandy. All there was, though, was vague supposition and a description of the major that might be any tallish, darkish man who looked as if he could handle himself in a fight. Perhaps, William thought, Fouché's famed intelligence network wasn't all it was made out to be. Perhaps Fouché controlled the population largely through fear – a belief that he knew everything whereas all he actually had was a few threads of gossip from which he wove a myth of omniscience.

William found himself wondering what information was going the other way. Why had some people been singled out for questioning? What did Fouché really know about daily life in Normandy? And did he have any inkling of the network moving British spies across the country?

As he thought about it, he realised that he had a way of discovering exactly what information was being sent back to Paris. Fouché's minions wore no uniforms and there were several couriers, so it stood to reason that new people must arrive all the time. Looking through the despatch case again, William turned up one sheet identifying the man – André Givernet – and authorising him to conduct enquiries and collect information for the State. If, William thought, he were to turn up in Dieppe, who was to say that he was not the courier? He could spend the afternoon snooping around, finding out where guards had been placed, learning who the police trusted as informants and who might be open to recruitment by the British. It was risky, of course, but was the risk really that great? The next morning he would be away, carrying with him all Dieppe's dirty little secrets to add to Fouché's files – only they would never get there. Somewhere between Dieppe and Paris, the courier would disappear with nothing to connect him to 'The Little Pig' or William Brown. It would be a small, but real, blow against Napoleon's France and it would leave him feeling that he was not completely wasting his time in Normandy.

He just hoped that after the hours listening to the girls at the Fleur Rouge his Parisian accent was up to the task he had set himself.

Once he had decided what he intended to do, he started off to Dieppe at once, before good sense took over and he thought better of it.

The barracks were easy enough to find. Once there, he adopted what he thought would be the tone of one of Fouché's men: arrogant and intimidatory.

127

Judging from the instant response and the salutes thrown by everyone from private to major, he had judged it right.

He was directed to a major's office where he threw down the despatch case. "Make sure the colonel sees these."

The major assured him that the papers would be with the colonel within the hour.

"And you have papers for me, for my return to Paris."

"They are being drawn up as we speak, sir."

William essayed a sneer. "Not ready yet, major?"

The major was sorry, the papers were almost ready. He had not expected that Monsieur – there was a pause while he looked for the letter of authority in the case – M Givernet would be leaving today.

"No, you are correct." William was condescending. "I leave tomorrow morning. Until then, I would like to see how the guard is being maintained on the coast. You will see from these papers that the Minister of Police is anxious that the tightest cordon is maintained."

It was, William thought, the sort of thing that Fouché's creatures would do and it had the advantage that it would allow him to scout out all the places that would have to be avoided when he and the major finally broke for the Channel. He reached over and took his letter of authority from the dispatch case. "Let your men know that I'll be around but I'll take this, just to be on the safe side."

It was as simple as that.

He spent the afternoon riding the countryside near the farm, making a note of the fixed guard posts, timing as best he could (he had no watch) the cavalry who patrolled now both day and night. As evening came on he decided to look at the *voltigeurs*. There was no particular reason for that, other than professional curiosity. *Voltigeurs* were roughly the equivalent of the English Rifle companies – although they would never be as good as the Rifles in his opinion. Still, it would be interesting to see how they moved through the woodland and how the officers kept control in the darkness between the trees.

He had to confess himself reluctantly impressed. Despite their ridiculous blue uniforms – so much less practical than the green of the Rifles – they merged into the shadows quite convincingly. Once he had almost ridden into one and a nervous lieutenant had hurried to assure the soldier that this was an important gentleman from Paris and not to be insulted.

William had almost decided to call it a night when there were shouts to his left. Turning his horse he went to see what all the excitement was about.

James Burke sat on his horse, his hands in the air and despair on his face.

CHAPTER 28: The last lap

"Who's the officer in charge?"

William's abrupt question brought a captain running.

"You are to be congratulated, captain. This is the fellow we've all been looking for. Now does anybody have some rope?"

There was some confusion until eventually one well-prepared corporal produced a length of rope. Burke's hands were duly tied and his feet were bound under the horse's belly. William took his horse's reins.

"I'm taking personal charge of this prisoner. I will start the interrogation tonight."

The captain tried to object: the man was dangerous; he needed a larger guard.

"Nonsense," insisted William. "He's tied and unarmed. He has information that is needed urgently in Paris. I can interrogate him tonight and I promise that long before dawn he will have told me all I want to know."

The captain's Adam's apple bobbed nervously. William's tone suggested that nobody wanted any details about how the interrogation would proceed.

William turned back toward Dieppe, leading Burke away at a smart trot.

"Impressive work," said Burke, when William had untied him and they were able to talk. "I owe you my life."

William mumbled something in which Burke could only make out the words 'nothing really'.

"It's true. And not for the first time." He looked around, trying to find some landmarks in the darkness. "The trouble is that they'll learn they have been fooled before morning and then they'll scour the countryside until we're found. I think my rescue is a strictly temporary measure and, worse, they'll be looking for you too now."

William nodded. "That's the bad news, certainly. The good news is that I know there's a group travelling out tomorrow night. So we only have to stay out of the Frenchies' grip for 24 hours. And I know their patrol routes and positions."

"That gives us a chance at any rate but we still need somewhere safe to lie up. We can't risk the cottage or the farm – they're both certain to be searched and we'd just be putting more lives at risk."

William sucked his teeth, like a tradesman about to inform you that the leak in your ceiling meant the whole roof would need to be repaired. "I'd suggest that we hide out in the woods, but those *voltigeurs* know their stuff. They might miss us, but they cover the ground pretty well."

As William spoke, Burke's expression was suddenly more hopeful. "The ground, William! They cover the ground, but what about –"

"The trees! Of course. They never look up, do they?"

Burke knew that William was thinking of when they had first known each other, hiding in a church tower while enemy troops had killed all their comrades on the ground below. It was true: they never looked up.

They abandoned the horses. Much as they would have welcomed the chance to ride for the sea once it became time to break cover, they could not risk tethering the animals anywhere near them.

They made their way through the wood, pausing every few seconds in case there were more *voltigeurs* lying in wait. Once they heard a branch snap. Perhaps it was a deer, but they lay silent for ten minutes to be on the safe side and then detoured away from the spot they thought the noise had come from.

Eventually, well away from any path, they found an oak. Burke remembered the story of King Charles hiding from the Roundheads in an oak tree and reckoned that if it worked for the king, it should work for them.

The lowest bough was something over six feet from the ground, which was a good thing as far as Burke was concerned because it meant that any passing searchers were that much less likely to see it as a possible hiding place.

With William making a stirrup of his hands to boost him up, Burke was able to get a grip on the branch above him and pull himself up onto the bough. He'd been sure to find a limb that was big enough for him to lay on it, gripping with his legs. Reaching down, he took hold of one of William's hands and pulled. He managed to lift him well clear of the ground, but he could not raise him to his own height.

They tried again. This time William turned to face the trunk and as soon as his feet were dangling in the air he swung himself to get a grip on the knobbly bark of the tree. As William swung, Burke thought his arms would wrench from their sockets, but he managed to hold on. He was beginning to sweat, despite the chill of the night, but William managed to take enough of his weight on his legs for Burke to lift him enough for his other hand to scrabble for its own grip on the bough.

Once William had a grip on the tree, it was only a matter of time. It didn't feel that straightforward to Burke, his muscles screaming, the tree digging into his body so that he thought he would have every whorl of the gnarled old oak printed on his chest for life. A few minutes later, though, they were both safely on the branch.

With the two of them there, they struggled to find space to settle and, besides, the bough had creaked alarmingly as it took the weight of both of them. Burke decided it would be safer if he climbed a little higher so they ended up settling on separate boughs where they tried to make themselves as comfortable as they could.

There was no question of sleep. Their perches were too insecure for it to be safe but in any case they stayed alert for every sound below. They heard men moving through the forest and once somebody passed right below the boughs where they were lying. By now, though, it was so dark that even if any of the searchers had looked up, they would have seen nothing.

The coming of dawn made them both feel more cheerful. They had, after all, survived the night. The day, though, brought new, and arguably more serious, problems. They had to take more care to lie still, concealed from anyone below. They were hungry and, above all, thirsty. And, though each knew the other was close by, they felt very alone. They could not see each other and dared not move so that they might. They dared not speak. Each just lay silent with their thoughts and waited for the night.

At one point they heard dogs and were terrified that they might set the beast loose in the wood where they were hidden, for surely the dogs would be able to find them. The animals were some way distant though and, as the afternoon wore on, their cries drifted further away.

At last the long day was over and dusk came to the forest. It was time to move.

This was, Burke knew, the most dangerous part of their escape. Once again they made their way through the trees, stopping and listening every few minutes. Progress was painfully slow, but they made it to the edge of the forest without being spotted.

It was a dark night. Occasionally a sliver of moon would be seen through gaps in the cloud. Burke blessed their good luck: enough light to navigate their way by, but dark enough to give them a chance of escaping the watching soldiers.

Burke followed William's lead. William led them round the spots where he knew there were likely to be guards. Soon the French would realise that they needed to change their positions, but it was unlikely that they had recognised the danger and had time to react already. Even so, every step they took away from the safety of the wood carried with it the danger of being seen.

It was a still night and every sound carried, meaning that they were constantly in fear of tripping in the dark or kicking a rock that rattled as it shifted. On the other hand, it made it easy to hear the cavalry patrols before they came near enough to have any chance of seeing them. Three times they heard hooves in the distance and lay pressed against the earth until the threat and vanished away. When the moon shone too brightly they would sink to the ground and crawl until it was dark enough for them to stand again.

An hour passed and they were still only half way to the cottage. Neither had a watch, but Burke began to worry they would not reach it in time.

There were, William assured him, few troops on the open country. The French relied instead on the cavalry patrols. Now they were a safe distance from the troops stationed along the margin of the wood they could move faster.

Ducking as low as they could, and praying there was no isolated sentry to spot them, they began to run towards where they thought they should find the cottage where they had first landed. After a quarter of an hour, Burke realised that they had no idea if they were even headed in the right direction.

"We're panicking. We need to stop and calm down."

William nodded. The two men lay alongside each other and waited for their breathing to slow. Once they were quiet Burke listened. There, in the distance, was the sound of waves breaking against the shore.

"We'll head this way. We walk: no more running. Stay calm and look out for anything that might be the cottage."

Burke was all too aware that he had never seen the cottage. He hoped that William's usually impressive sense of direction did not let them down.

After ten minutes of walking, William spoke. "Judging from the sound of the waves, I reckon we're about the right distance from the shore and the cottage should be to the north of here, though I can't be certain."

Burke didn't like the sound of that 'can't be certain'. If William was wrong, they would be walking away from the cottage, not towards it. And every minute brought them closer to the time that the boat would arrive to take off the Alien Office's agents. If they missed that boat, their chances of survival did not bear thinking about.

They walked for, as far as Burke could judge, another ten minutes with no sign of the cottage. No light broke the darkness; there was no sound save the waves breaking against the cliffs.

Even if they were walking in the right direction, perhaps their escape was still doomed. Suppose the French had searched the cottage? Suppose Etienne and his wife were already on their way to Paris, to meet Fouché in the *Tour Bonbec*?

He had not slept for thirty hours nor eaten for over 24. William had had a water flask which they had shared, but he was thirsty now. He stumbled on in the dark, William stumbling beside him.

In his fatigue he began to hallucinate. He saw horses riding towards him and was about to throw himself to the ground when he realised that there was no sound of hoof beats. The horses were a creation of his exhausted brain. He imagined the masts of a ship towering over the cliffs and struggled to imagine how they could reach so high towards the sky. He thought he saw Amelie walking beside William.

He thought he saw the shape of a cottage in the darkness ahead of them.

* * *

They recognised William and hurried to help them both to seats. There was food and water and friendly voices. No, they had seen no soldiers nearby. Burke thanked his guardian angel that William had destroyed the order to search the cottage and that the hunt for them was still inland or south toward Dieppe. Etienne must be warned that they could bring no-one ashore tonight: the days to come would see too much activity from the French. They just needed to get the agents out and go to ground until things grew quieter.

He was not to worry, Etienne assured him as his wife poured more soup, they would deal with everything. He and William must rest for an hour and then the boat would arrive.

The hour passed quickly, Burke slipping in and out of a sleep so deep that the French could have hammered on the door and they wouldn't have woken him. In time, though, Etienne shook him gently awake and they started the last half mile of their journey home.

Etienne carried a pistol and his wife accompanied them. If they ran into trouble, he would shoot if necessary and then they would flee with the others to England. "But I expect no trouble," he said confidently. "They seldom patrol here, trusting to the cliffs to guard the coast better than any soldiers could."

He was right. Although everyone was on edge, starting at every sound, real or imagined, they reached the cliffs without incident. Then there was the descent. Burke, of course, had been spared the climb up. Looking down now, he couldn't imagine pulling himself up the rope in the dark. Going down was bad enough, his arms, still sore from lifting William into the oak, were screaming in agony before he was half way down. Twice he had to stop, wrapping his arms and legs around the rope while he summoned up the strength to continue.

At last he was on the ground and hands reached to help him into the boat grounded on the beach.

"Push out."

He felt the hull bobbing on the water and then the men were at the oars and they were heading out towards the *Basilisk* and England.

CHAPTER 29: The *Basilisk*

Burke and William stood on the deck of the *Basilisk* and watched France slipping away into the darkness. The bosun had ordered them to the cabin but Burke had suggested that he might like to reconsider that idea. The bosun had seemed about to argue, but one look at the expression on Burke's face made him reconsider and he developed a sudden interest in the trimming of the sails.

Despite having spent most of the previous 24 hours in close proximity, this was the first opportunity that the two had had any chance for conversation and both were understandably anxious to know about the other's adventures. Burke was sure that as soon as they were back in England the Alien Office would escort them back to London and then Colonel Gordon would expect a report and their conversation was hardly suitable for a London tavern. The deck of the *Basilisk* offered as much opportunity for privacy as they were likely to see for a while.

Somehow – Burke had no idea how and didn't want to know – William had managed to liberate a generous portion of naval rum. Their talk started as a rehearsal of the basic facts of their journeys that could usefully form the basis of Burke's report, but as the ship moved further into the channel and the rum did its work, their accounts become steadily less coherent and dwelt more on the personal aspects of their adventures. William even became drunk enough to admit how he was smuggled out of the brothel, while Burke explained how Amelie and Josephine had sheltered him in the Tuileries.

"We can be proud of what we did, William. The Alien Office won't be sending any more agents to that inn. We saved the three of them, tweaked Fouché's nose and you've even got intelligence on Fouché's network in Normandy. A job well done, I think."

They toasted each other in rum.

"And a toast to Ma'amselle Pascale," said Burke. "You fell on your feet with that one. She sounds a remarkable woman."

William took another healthy swig of the rum. "She was, sir. She was something special."

"And did you…?"

William looked shocked. "No sir, wouldn't be my place." He thought for a bit, he face screwed up with the concentration of the seriously inebriated. "But the Empress, sir? I mean, she's married to Napoleon. You didn't…?"

Burke was very drunk by then but still managed to maintain a semblance of dignity as he wagged an admonishing finger at William.

"You shouldn't be asking that, William. Remember, William, a gentleman never tells." And he fell back against the bulwarks and slept.

"But an Empress…" William struggled to make sense of their adventure. He drained the mug of liberated rum. They were alive. They were on their way back to London and his Molly. All was right with the world. He slumped down alongside the major.

The bosun, drawn by their snoring, was about to wake them when the captain tapped him on the shoulder. Etienne had spoken to the crew of the ship's boat while they waited for Burke to climb down the rope and the captain had put two and two together.

"Leave them be, bosun."

The boson sniffed. The smell of rum was all too obvious. "They're drunk, sir."

"They are fine men, bosun. Tired, perhaps. But I'm sure they aren't drunk."

William snored and belched rum fumes in his sleep.

"Very tired," said the captain. "Leave them be."

HISTORICAL NOTE

When I was very young I read and enjoyed Baroness Orczy's Scarlet Pimpernel stories. Recently I re-read *The Triumph of the Scarlet Pimpernel*. I thought it was a fun read but I had my doubts about some of the history. The melodramatic way in which Robespierre is toppled by an eloquent speech from someone trying to save his mistress's life seemed to be quite unbelievable. Except, of course, that it (or something very like it) actually happened. Incredible as it seems, that scene is probably the most historically accurate bit of the whole book.

The lesson is that even an outrageous historical romp can involve much more research than the reader (and probably even the writer) ever expected.

So it has been with *Burke and the Pimpernel Affair*. After the grim (and tightly written as far as the historical facts go) *Burke in Ireland*, the idea was to write a frothy Bond-style thriller with no major historical incidents in it and thus rather less need for research than most of the books in the series. It didn't quite work out that way.

The Alien Office did run agents into France much as described. The chain of safe houses may have been changed by 1809 but I've stolen a lot of the detail from Tim Clayton's *This Dark Business* which describes the running of agents in 1803.

I've seen the Conciergerie from outside, but I had no idea of its significance and, sadly, I couldn't visit while I was writing the book because of Covid restrictions. It didn't make that much difference from the point of view of research, as the building was substantially remodelled in the 19th century and much of an earlier draft had to be rewritten when I realised that even the exterior was now dramatically different from what it had been in 1809. The details of the infirmary and the cells (where Marie Antoinette really was imprisoned) are extrapolated from the accounts I could find of the appearance of the place then, including one account of another gaol break. It does seem to have been surprisingly easy to get out of.

Malmaison still exists and I look forward to visiting one day when international travel is less of an adventure. Fortunately there are some excellent virtual walk-throughs online, though none feature the menagerie, which is no longer there.

Fouché does seem to have been a very unpleasant person, and I say that based not on the words of his enemies but on his own memoirs, which show that the badly written self-justifying political memoir has been around for much longer than you might think. And he really did plot to encourage Napoleon's divorce.

I can't swear that I've been entirely fair to Josephine but I think the picture I've painted of her fits much that is known about her personality. I think I'd have liked her if I'd met her. (She seemed to have that effect on men.) She almost certainly met Burke, though earlier than 1809. He managed to infiltrate her court while Napoleon was absent on military business.

The Vicomte Morel de Vindé was also a real person and his survival through the Terror and his studies in agronomy are true. He seems to have been an interesting chap.

As to the rest: I've spent far too long reading about things like the organisation of the *gendarmerie* and looking at fashion plates in magazines of the time and even checking out the costumes in the V&A museum in London. But you don't need to worry about all that. I just want you to enjoy a very silly story that, it turns out, is not, perhaps, as silly as it might be.

And that sudden warm spell that let William enjoy his picnic with the girls from the Fleur Rouge? It really happened.

Thank you

Writing is, by its nature, a solitary exercise but there are lots of people who contribute to the finished product. Somehow, *Burke and the Pimpernel Affair* seems to have drawn in more people than usual.

Thanks first to my wife, Tammy. This is traditional, I know, but in her case especially well-deserved. She is not only generally supportive of my writing but she listens to me reading key sections aloud. She is the first to see my draft copies and she is happy to praise the bits she thinks work and to savage the bits that don't. She also proof reads with the dedication of someone who was diagnosed dyslexic as a child and has fought through by checking and re-checking her own work and, now, my efforts.

My son gets pulled in for comments before anyone but Tammy has seen it and then come beta readers. Readers for this one included Paul Benedyk (who would make a wonderful professional proof-reader), John Haines and Stacy Townend.

I'm particularly grateful to Jane Pollard, who brings a lifetime of experience to encouraging me to strengthen my female characters and build the intensity of emotional scenes. Jane has retired from writing, which is a huge loss to the world of historical romantic fiction where she wrote as Jane Jackson. Her back catalogue is still available online and I would encourage you to take a look at it.

The errors that remain and the bits you don't like are, of course, entirely down to me.

Cover design is by Dave Slaney. Dave does all my books and is very, very good at it.

My thanks go to everyone who helped and to you, dear reader, for supporting me with your attention. And special thanks to those of you who go online to Amazon or Goodreads and leave a review. Reviews are not just gratifying to authors (we do like to think people have enjoyed what we write) but also invaluable in generating sales. We're not looking for literary essays – just a sentence or two will help.

Burke will be back ...

I hope you have enjoyed *Burke and the Pimpernel Affair.* This is the sixth book about James Burke. Do take a look at the others if you haven't already. They haven't been written in chronological order so you can read them in whatever order you want, but the first is *Burke in the Land of Silver* which is the one most closely based on the real James Burke's life (yes, he really existed) so it's an obvious place to start.

If you want to learn more about the books and the world that James Burke lived in, I recommend that you have a look at my website: http://tomwilliamsauthor.co.uk where you can sign up to my newsletter and be the first to hear about new books. You can also follow me on Facebook (https://www.facebook.com/AuthorTomWilliams) and Twitter (https://twitter.com/TomCW99).

I'm sure you've seen notes from authors before asking that you review their books on Amazon, but it really makes a huge difference. Without a big marketing budget (and hardly any authors are given those), Amazon reviews are crucial to getting books to an audience. If you have enjoyed *Burke and the Pimpernel Affair* and would like other people to have a chance to enjoy it too, it would be so helpful if you could write a few words on Amazon. Just a sentence or two saying that you liked it and you think others might is all it takes – we're not talking about the Times Literary Supplement here. I do read all my reviews (writers who say they don't are almost certainly fibbing) and I love getting them.

Thank you again for reading.

OTHER BOOKS BY TOM WILLIAMS

James Burke, spy

Burke in the Land of Silver

Burke and the Bedouin

Burke at Waterloo

Burke in the Peninsula

Burke in Ireland

The Williamson Papers

The White Rajah

Cawnpore

Back Home

Contemporary Urban Fantasy

Dark Magic

Something Wicked

Printed in Great Britain
by Amazon

80120555R00088